PHILIPPA'S FOLLY

PHILIPPA'S FOLLY

Louise Couper

POOLBEG

Published 1996 by
Poolbeg Press Ltd,
123 Baldoyle Industrial Estate,
Dublin 13, Ireland
Reprinted 1996

A catalogue record for this book is available from the British Library.

ISBN 1 85371 543 3

Cover painting Late Summer by Stephen Darbishire
By courtesy of Richard Hagen Ltd, Yew Tree House.
Broadway, Worcestershire WR12 7DT
Cover design by Poolbeg Group Services Ltd
Set by Poolbeg Group Services Ltd in Goudy
Printed and bound in Great Britain by
Cox & Wyman Ltd, Reading, Berkshire.

A note on the author

Louise Couper was born in Dublin and graduated from TCD. She now lives with her husband and two sons on an organic farm in Co Westmeath.

Her first novel, *Philippa's Farm* was a winner of the Eason Discovery Award 1995 for the best up and coming writers of modern fiction.

For Grant and Colin

Marriage

of

Philippa Woodcock
formerly of Philippa's Farm, Slieve Blooms,
Ireland

to

Gerald Ransome
of Woodleigh Hall, Norwich, England

on

21 June 1995

You are cordially invited to the above nuptials
Reception in The Imperial Hotel, Ballinamore

RSVP   *Strictly formal*
– Don't bother, just come. P.

⚜ Chapter One ⚜

Honeymoons are like a cool drink on a hot day – you'd like to savour it but you're so damn thirsty you gulp the whole lot in one go. I tried to feign shyness, a slight indifference even, though such subterfuge was one of the greatest trials of my life. In the end, my animal instincts got the better of me.

"Would you like to stop to catch your breath, Pips?" Gerald asked anxiously.

"If that's what *you* want," I replied.

"Well . . . I'm asking *you* what *you'd* like."

So anyway, we paused, let the room stop spinning and had the rest of the champagne.

Of course it was Gerald's first time.

"I simply never found anyone I liked well enough to be that intimate with," he'd said in the bluebell wood all those months ago. However, any doubts I'd had about his sexual prowess quickly vanished in that tiny bedroom in Rome. All those old wives' tales about men having to practice and sow a few wild oats were utter rubbish. Gerald knew exactly what to do as if it had been encoded in his genes.

"But the judo – when on earth . . . ?" I asked.

"Just before I took off on my lonely trek to the Himalayas. I thought it might come in useful against thieves as I trudged across glaciers in the cool of night."

"You're joking!"

"Only slightly. No point in being a writer if you can't enjoy yourself."

He sat up and leant on his elbow.

"One thing puzzles me though . . ."

"What's that, Gerald?"

"How on earth does a man-eating tiger happen to be alive and well on the Capitoline Hill?"

I gave my very best snarl. "She just kept a very low prrrr-o-file."

Fortunately I'd brought my honeymoon "tool kit" to soothe love's abrasions when tender spots get even more tender and while that particular discomfort has its animal joys up to a point, no sense in being a martyr. Gerald ran a bath twice a day and with the most gentle of touches, smoothed away any muscle trauma.

"Is that where it hurts?" he asked in his most concerned voice as he rubbed my aching limbs up to my thighs and even higher, if I was lucky.

"Yes, quite a bit. That's it, a little higher, a tiny bit harder. Yes. Yes . . ."

And, of course, we'd be off again, animals that we are, taking delight in an act designed to make procreation a pleasure, otherwise who would bother? Nothing like it for taking the mind off pigs, sheep, relations and friends.

The wedding itself was the usual expensive, nerve-wrecking business with each side eyeing the other, determined to find fault, though of course this was more on Gerald's side than mine. Eddie, having saved her from herself during her last serious bout of the DT's, was the centre of my sister Aggie's attention — shared only with the champagne. My brother Andy, still looking as if fresh from the Australian outback, spent his time listening to the mad ravings of Gloria, his girlfriend. Not the slightest bit of attention was paid to me, but this was par for the Woodcocks.

Aggie, in her haste to don her distinctly unflattering plumes of coral chiffon, "forgot" to collect my bouquet of flowers and pay the organist at the church. We very nearly had a silent wedding march until good old Noreen of the archaeological society tore up the narrow steps to the choir and put a twenty pound note into the organist's hand. Then we had Vidor's *Toccata* with a vengeance. Aggie threatened to sing in her soprano without the gin, which would have cleared the church; with gin, would simply have meant a slight headache or a fit of the giggles, depending on your nature. I'm the giggly type. Hugely irritating for the onlooker but enormous fun to the partaker.

The ceremony was simple and straightforward, as befits the marriage contract.

"Contrary to what most people think," Eddie, my ex of long ago, informed me by telephone in the dead of night, "the thing you sign is a contract for sex."

I wasn't complaining. That was at least half the fun.

"So long as it isn't life-threatening, Eddie, I'm sure it'll be all right."

"Why do you need a piece of paper to do that? It's all a bureaucratic swizz to keep tabs on you and your offspring. There is such a thing as commitment you know."

I didn't bother explaining that I liked bits of paper, like marriage lines, house deeds and land certificates.

A dozen of those photos that in time grow yellow and dog-eared and bore the pants off visitors were taken in front of the apple trees at my little farm before we set off: Gerald and me looking lovingly into our various orbs; Gerald and Pimmsy, his father; Gerald and me and Pimmsy; Aggie, my one and only sister and me; Aggie and my brother Andy; Aggie, Andy and Me – in that order. Aggie insisted on standing in front to show the world her dress, or what there was of it. The Wonderbra did its best.

"Better be Big Sis Sybil next, or she'll 'get the hump' as you so elegantly put it," Gerald said.

Sybil looked as though she had several humps already, and like so many voluminous women, she had married a diminutive, though perfectly formed, person by the name of Sheepshanks.

"You can't be serious, Gerald," I shrieked when I heard her name. Old Mutton Chops suited her better.

She thrust herself towards the camera in her striking regalia – shimmering archbishop purple with enormous cabbage roses at the waist – she pulled a skinny child alongside.

Gerald said, "They *say* it's theirs but I can't imagine Sybil . . ."

I looked at him.

"You know . . . Philippa! You know perfectly well what I mean!"

PJ, my next door neighbour, laid on his jeep – specially washed free of cow dung for the occasion – and the Ransomes clambered in. Gerald and I had a surreptitious glass of champers by the cocktail cabinet before we sped off to the church.

"I wish you'd say what those eyes *seem* to be saying, or is it the bubbly?" I asked.

He got all serious then. "Well, Pips, just thinking how much I love you."

Nothing guaranteed to floor a girl more on her wedding day.

"Gosh, Pips. What is it?"

My eyes burned and snot trickled down my nose. Great.

He pulled a dazzling white hankie from his pocket. "Here, let me." And dabbed at my eyes and wiped my nose. "What an ogre, making a girl cry on her wedding day."

"It's just that . . ." I wanted to explain something about being loved, that it was such a change, that I wasn't used to it, but the tears boiled down and the snot flowed even more freely.

"Here let me take your glass. Let's relax for a minute."

Gerald led me towards my Provencal couch. It clashed horribly with my beautiful ivory dress, like a scone with champagne. My teeth chattered; my body seemed something apart. The tears had stopped.

"Maybe I'm coming down with flu."

Gerald lifted my chin and examined my eyes.

"Looks like good old-fashioned fear to me."

Writers think they know everything.

"Never was frightened of anything in my life," I protested. But as honest words have a habit of doing, it sank home. I couldn't think of a single clever or cheeky thing to say.

We reached the church at last. The guests seemed unsettled, obviously fed up waiting. I smoothed my dress as best I could. Gaye Greene, having made the dress, had managed to come to the wedding, though still in the throes of recovering from the usual childbirth joys of high blood pressure, threatened toxaemia, painful induction, episiotomy, forceps, stitches, engorged breasts, a severe bout of mastitis and a screaming baby.

"But it really doesn't matter," she had lied. "So long as the baby is OK."

"It would still have been all right in spite of all those things, Gaye."

She lifted my ivory silk creation over my head for the final fitting. She could just have told me to shut up.

Out came the antique cheval mirror.

I *was* speechless. Gaye had turned a bolt of fabric into a work of art. The full skirt, gathered at my wasp-like waist, was balanced at the shoulders by sleeves made from three layers of fabric, each one shorter than the other. The neckline was clean and wide, though not plunging.

"I think a broad belt of the same material gathered into a large bow at the back will finish it off."

I praised her gift with the scissors.

"When you've got a good body to work on – and yours is a dressmaker's dream – it's easy."

I never argue with an expert.

By the time the reception came round, we were ravenous. Sybil got the show on the road. She ordered the waiters around and ensured her wine glass was kept topped up, except for the few seconds she took to shake Gerald's hand and wish him well. To me she cast a doubtful look, which I ignored. Her husband Henry ladled peanuts and crisps into himself as if he had just come off a desert island. Their daughter, on the other hand, looked as though she never ate a bite, first cousin, physically speaking, to Anorexia, my "spinning" acquaintance from Bath.

Gerald's father, "Pimmsy" to his friends, for reasons which were rapidly becoming clear, was hurriedly "replenishing the moisture lost on the horrendous journey to Ireland", though this probably had more to do with the company of his daughter than with the B & I crossing.

"Had my first taste of a Pimms when I was a lad of sixteen," he told me with the merest hint of a slur.

"Hollow legs," Gerald whispered.

"Afraid Papa may have Alzheimer's or some form of memory loss," Mrs Mutton confided to me. "I'm sure he'll be well looked after now that Gerald has finally realised where his duty lies. Poor Papa needs to be taken care of."

Indeed. Nothing that a slight curtailing of his drink ration wouldn't cure. Of course, I kept my mouth shut.

"He needs plenty of milk puddings and poached fish," she added, sucking her glass dry.

"Only if you think he really should have all those dairy hormones and plutonium-glowing fish," I said.

She ran to refill her glass.

Pimmsy got on with Noreen's Seamus like a house on fire, *ça va sans dire*. So many drinking stories to tell each other – and for the first time! Not an opportunity that comes often in a lifetime.

"A grand man," Seamus confided, on his way to the bar with two empty glasses.

"Your type, Seamus?" I smiled.

"Well, to be honest a bit English, but you can forgive that when he has such a bad time with the gout and the tenants and has trouble deciding where to invest the few pound."

Seamus's tolerance level was seemingly stratospheric. I made a mental note to introduce him to old Mutton Chops.

"I suppose we all have our problems," I said to him, looking at no one in particular. "Is your dear wife hereabouts?" I enquired, before he got his riposte in.

"I saw her and Emily slip upstairs to help Gaye Greene with the babby. Never saw anything so fussed over. Spoiled. He'll grow up a sissy."

"What do you recommend, Seamus? Smacking and starvation?"

I knew I'd gone a bit far but I was cross. The poor child needed all the comfort and attention it could muster.

He gave me a dirty look and slid off to tell another hilarious yarn to Pimmsy.

We'd picked the Imperial in Ballinamore for the reception as Aggie knew the manager. Or said she did. It turned out they were in the same drying-out clinic together. While the menu had offered perfectly acceptable dishes, they arrived on the table looking completely transformed and tasting uniquely disgusting. The turkey had obviously given itself up, and the ham – pink indiarubber, expanding as you chewed. Pudding was delivered with the usual panache that accompanies that most overrated of dishes, Baked Alaska. Unfortunately, Alaska had suffered a sudden heatwave, and its mountain of froth had slithered to one side. Someone ate it, however, as Gerald and I counted as least two empty platters on their way back to the kitchen. By the time coffee arrived, I could contain myself no longer and shot Aggie a withering look.

"Don't worry, Pips. It won't cost you a farthing."

Which was all very fine but Gerald and I were still hungry. Perhaps, if I said my goodbyes now, we could slip away unnoticed . . .

I made my way up the stairs to see Noreen and

Gaye Greene with her new baby. They were ensconced in a large Victorian bedroom, with flowery wallpaper and faded red velvet curtains. Emily Delaney was there too, a tight look to her mouth, born of lack of affection.

"Pips!" Gaye Greene shrieked at the sight of me. "How is married bliss?"

"So far, so good. Time alone will tell."

"But you've a grand man there, Philippa," Noreen said. "I'll take him off your hands when you're fed up of him." She blew a stream of smoke into the air, delighted with her little joke.

"Baby's getting a baptism of fire," I said quietly, my eyes on the cigarette.

"Sure didn't I rear a clutch of them and they can all breathe and drink porter," she said a little too defensively, I felt. However, Noreen is no respecter of time or place.

Gaye was cross.

"They very kindly let me have the room to feed little Tommy in! Probably so I wouldn't terrify the clientele. Strange how the sight of a woman feeding a baby seems to send shock waves throughout the country. Yet when bare breasts are dangled on the third page of a newspaper, it seems to be all right!"

Something to do with the male unwillingness to share their toy perhaps. I wisely said nothing, of course.

"You wouldn't even know you were doing it!" Noreen broke the silence.

"You just open a button and plug him on. Nothing to it," Gaye replied, smiling at me.

"Well, Philippa. It'll be your turn soon," Noreen said in that silly tone of hers, reserved for donkeys on beaches to urge them along.

"Afraid I'd be useless to the poor little mite, Noreen."

"I don't mean that! I mean when you and that nice husband of yours produce a little fellow in about nine month's time."

"That's in the lap of the Gods," I replied curtly.

The truth was I'd have liked a baby immediately. But first things first.

"Never could do that," Emily said gesturing towards the baby suckling his mother. "Could never get it into my head that that's what they were for."

The mind boggled. Perhaps breasts will become a thing of the genetic past, like the third eye or prehensile grip. The death of the porn industry. More unemployment.

"Sure isn't that what Himself made them for," Noreen said quietly, stubbing out the cigarette. "Best milk on this earth for rearing a baby. All them packages are made from cow's milk, fine for a calf but, if you want brains, it has to be the breast."

Must be what happened to Seamus. Mother went dry.

"That's right, Noreen. Percy and I read that mother's milk was designed to make the cells in the brain grow. Babies reared by their mothers have heavier brains than packet-reared ones," Gaye said, looking the picture of maternal fulfilment as she lay back on the pillows.

"All the same," Emily said wistfully, "I couldn't do it. Would have put Dickie off sex for life if he'd seen that," she said pointing to mother and child.

It looked as if that happened anyway, if the caresses of Dickie and Percy I witnessed in Antibes were anything to go by. Entwined like convolvulous. But if Emily seemed blind to Dickie's propensities, Gaye had no illusions about Percy.

"Well girls," Noreen said, gathering her vast handbag and smoothing down her ample curves. "There's dancing and music downstairs if you want to lose some of the flab. *Hunky Hank and the Red Necks* are playing."

Just what I needed.

To get the ball rolling, the Imperial laid on a foursome to do some set dancing. Though cheerful and charming, the céilí dancers were long past the age when bosoms were elastic enough to take a jig or two. It was now a question of mountains of flesh heaving up, down or sideways. Breasts were tossed about with abandon. Pimmsy and Seamus were riveted. I wanted to tell them to take a good look, they might soon become a thing of the past, when Gerald appeared beside me.

"Enjoying yourself, Philippa?" he asked me.

"Of course," I lied.

"In that case, perhaps we could slip away and have a glass of something cold I sneaked into your fridge."

We had ignored the age-old superstition about it being unlucky for the bride and groom to catch sight of each other the day of the nuptials. Gerard slept chastely in the pink room, not the least bit nervous or abashed or even mildly concerned about the "bed" part of the whole proceedings.

"I like you, Philippa. That's all that matters," he replied in response to my oblique enquiries about "it".

What happened at my little farm that night when we had finished the bottle of champagne, *Philippa's Pâté* on thinly sliced home-made brown bread, followed by the aphrodisiacal *spinster's cake* with rose icing, only the Gods of Love would understand. I thought I had a reasonable body before then; that night I realised just how wonderful it was. Mother always said that a good man could do wonders for a woman, though she probably meant boxes of chocolates and bunches of flowers. Who needs them when there's the gift of intimacy?

What was merely the prelude on our wedding night, became a complete symphony in Rome with days of culture and nights of rupture.

The mornings were taken up with visits to the usual tourist haunts, though we escaped the depredations of the thieves, who seem to outnumber tourists by two to one. There are always two of them on a motor bike, chopping bags off at the shoulder. Anyone who resists is merely dragged along the street. Plays havoc with a good tan. In fact, the reason the Italian leather industry is doing a bomb is because the tourists have to replace all the stolen handbags.

The Sistine Chapel was a let-down. Restoration had absolutely ruined it, rendering the frescoes glamorous and picture-postcardy. Gone were Michaelangelo's subtleties. The slides looked infinitely better. People of every nationality and hue crowding together in the hot, stuffy room with their heads thrown back were infinitely more engaging than the Michaelangelos. Amazing the types of chins and necks people wear.

A tape recorder came on every ten minutes to tell everyone to "shut up" in seven languages. Every breath and voice vibration apparently wrecks the paintwork, causing it to peel or go mouldy. Perhaps one day it will all come down. Yet another place from which humanity with its eggy breath and thudding feet will be banned like the Parthenon, the Caves of Lascaux and Stonehenge.

"Lunch?" Gerald whispered as soon as the shutting up voice came on the airwaves once again.

I nodded.

"You can tell a good Italian restaurant from a mediocre one by its napkins. The good ones use cloth, not paper." Gerald was a mine of information.

It was a cloth-using restaurant we found, with a ten page menu.

Gerald ordered the *vitello alla sarda* and I decided on the *cannelloni con salsa spinaci*. And of course a bottle of chianti.

"You've a good appetite, Gerald," I remarked as an entire plateful was quickly despatched with half a dozen fork-loads.

"Do I detect a note of criticism there?"

I bridled. "Merely an observation. No need to be so prickly."

"I don't hear myself make rude remarks about the way you eat. Married less than a week and already you want to change me."

"Nothing could be further from the truth. I resent that remark. I'm the easiest-going person alive. If you had a brother like mine for a stable-mate, you'd know all about bad table manners."

"So now I'm like that refugee from the Australian outback!"

I was floored. I pushed my plate away, ill at the thought of eating what only minutes before I'd relished. Was this really happening? Gerald turning into a monster – and so soon? One hears of couples married for forty years finally having enough of their snoring, or squeezing the toothpaste tube in the middle or eating with their mouth open, and deciding to go on separate holidays. But four days . . . !

Even the wine had gone sour. Perhaps it was all that walking about that did it. Tired him out so he could no longer be civil. Gerald now seemed English to the core: cold, distant and arrogant.

The waiter cleared the table, glancing from Gerald to me and back again.

"Dolci?" he enquired.

I shook my head and didn't bother to see what my late husband had decided. Perhaps Eddie had a point about not bothering with certificates and officialdom. Much easier to walk away.

"Frutta?" the waiter's voice went up an octave.

Minutes later an enormous white bowl full of fruit – grapes, peaches, nectarines and cherries – was placed between us.

I didn't budge.

Gerald set to with knife and plate and peeled and sliced and ate until the bowl was empty. It obviously took some momentous event, like death, to put Gerald off his food. How could I have been so stupid as to marry someone like him, who relished his food even though I was miserable? I thought he loved me. I really was fooled. Obviously love has nothing to do with intelligence. I could take the first plane, get a taxi from the airport and be home within eight hours. I could pretend the marriage was unconsummated and get an annulment within a year. The Church would be most anxious that I would re-marry quickly so as to bring as many children as possible into the world before the ovaries gave up the ghost.

"Coffee?" I heard a voice very like Gerald's emerge from a dark tunnel.

I refused.

"Oh, go on. They have some very nice truffles to go with it."

That was a different matter. I assented. Nothing like hot coffee and melting chocolate to make a girl glad to be alive.

"Sorry if I got a bit cross," he said lifting my hand and pressing his cherry-stained lips to it. "My mother was a devil about food. Wasn't interested in it herself and thought no one else should be. I was lucky to get a decent plateful. So, I tend to make a pig of myself whenever possible – just to show her."

Strange how the agonies of only a few moments can melt like snow off a ditch when the sun shines. I was already feeling sorry for the crabby bugger.

"I've no objection to you eating to your heart's content, Gerald. I'm not your mother."

"That's true, Philippa. She didn't have your

wonderful . . ." He cast his eyes appreciatively over my every curve.

" . . . Mind."

I slipped a truffle down his Jerymn Street shirt. One from his dish, of course.

After a few days of the dizzy splendours of Rome, we retired to the sunshine and waves of Sorrento.

"Let's not bother unpacking and go for a swim instead. Don't know about you, I could do with a cool bath."

We took everything off, saw how wonderful we both looked and celebrated it with an hour in bed.

"You know, Gerald, every time we make love we should have the possibility of children forever in our minds – or wherever."

"Rather a lot of children, I imagine. Whose crackpot notion is that?"

"None other than the Church, which says that if we make love merely for pleasure, it robs the act of its human dignity."

"Sounds like they're confusing lust and love. Surely an act performed with love, even or especially if that includes pleasure, can't be unchristian?" He pulled on his togs. "I would find it impossible to make love unless I really liked the person; loved the person." He kissed me on the tip of the nose. "Sex itself never appealed to me. You can do it just as well yourself and you don't have to worry about VD. With two people, it's love that makes the difference."

I didn't know what I did to deserve such a wonderful person.

The beach was a steep climb down a cliff – no joke when you're lugging filled rolls and a couple of bottles of wine. However, when we saw the sea, we felt it was almost worth it. The waves crashed magnificently as the water pushed its way up the beach and then tore at the sand and anyone else in its path as it made its way out again.

"Bit of an undertow there," Gerald mused.

Not my *tasse de thé*, being drowned while on holiday.

"I'll just lie in the sun and let you brave the elements," I said.

I spread a large towel on the sand and, of course, my pillow. Though it took up a large amount of luggage space, I was determined not to leave home without it. Foreign hotels never seem to have feather pillows and who wants to lie in someone else's sleepy slear anyway? Apparently they are so awash with tiny bugs who feed on the feathers and wax lyrical in saliva, that a pillow can move of its own accord! Not to mention duvets. It explains why pillows end up in a tight ball at the top of the bed while the duvet slips onto the floor. Just the bugs having a gay old time. The only cure is to have two pillows and a freezer. One pillow is in the freezer, week about, to kill off the bugs. Although in winter, three is more practical as the spare can be thawing while the others are either freezing or walking.

Gerald was the picture of health in his bright yellow shorts and English skin. He did have hair on his chest, which was important to us girls at school but I must admit did nothing much for me now. I can't for the life of me see the attraction. Perhaps it's to do with something to cling to that satisfies the primitive brain. Maybe some women find the chest ticklish against their bosom. Can't say I've noticed, though it's worth a try.

"Do you enjoy having hair on your chest?" I asked the dripping vision of manhood on his return from the sea.

Gerald seemed a bit startled by the question.

"Well, there's not much I can do about it. Comes with the rest of the kit and caboddle."

"You could shave it off," I suggested.

"Would you really like me to?" He seemed deadly serious, almost anxious for my approval.

"Well, I did say 'for better or worse'."

A bikini full of sand is *horrible*.

The Italians on holiday were a treat to watch. The young people pranced up and down the beach in variously provocative poses, leaving little to the imagination. According to the local papers, the sale of tissues at holiday resorts reaches an all-time high as young men press them into shape to enhance what nature has left wanting. The difficulties arise when they leap in for a swim.

By mid-afternoon, I was hot enough to feel an urge to get wet.

"It's as warm as a bath," Gerald encouraged, taking my hand.

And so it was. We rolled in the swollen waves like embryos in a womb, though without the advantage of the umbilical cord to haul you back to *terra firma* when the life was practically scared out of you. However, in spite of the dangers, real or fanciful, there is something primevally soothing about lolling around in water, being carried along without effort. We lay on our backs, holding each other, giving ourselves up to the power of the Universe.

"Do you know, Gerald, I think there might be a God after all," I said between waves.

"Did you ever doubt it?"

"When you're herded into a church each week, not to mention paraded around on hot Sundays following a banner of some sacred personage or another, it tends to dampen your enthusiasm for the spiritual."

Not to mention all the taboos about sex — though I didn't mention these to Gerald in case he realised what a naughty girl I was.

We visited Pompeii – so that I could tell the archaeological society the honeymoon was not unalloyed pleasure. Our guide, in an effort to help the tourists feel at home, was dressed in a fringed safari jacket and Stetson. He pointed his little plastic gun at us and pulled the trigger. A cloth descended with "Bang Bang" written on it.

"Do we really have to go, Philippa?" Gerald whispered.

I nodded. "Now you know why we'd to pay in advance."

"Pompeii is waiting you," Bang Bang smiled and ushered us onto a bus, already crammed with tourists.

Terrific.

No sooner had we left Sorrento than Bang Bang burst into *Todrna a Sorrento* followed by *Funiculi Funicula*.

"Really, Philippa. Couldn't we have hired a car?"

"Even more dangerous on these roads than being on a tour bus," I replied and mercifully dozed off.

The bus disgorged us two hours later. Hundreds of other people had decided to visit the ruins the same day. As Goethe said, never has such a disaster provided so much entertainment for posterity. The inhabitants of the town were shown in various stages of capture by the volcanic dust either retrieving their jewellery or taking a bath, though, surprisingly, no one in *flagranté*. So much for the myth about the Italians being such wonderful lovers. Perhaps it all happened at lunchtime when there was something more important to do, like eat.

"Looks like London after the Blitz," one of our number declared staring at the ruins. Gerald groaned.

We were led through the narrow, carriage-rutted streets, past the oldest pizzeria known, shown jars of fish sauce from the factory of Umbricus Agathopus. Who says the entrepreneur was born in the 20th century?

Crocodile fashion we entered the House of the Vettii. Once we had been shown the murals and courtyards of the famous brothers, the women were allowed to wander outside, while Bang Bang winked at Gerald and the other men to see something *speciale*. I cocked an ear.

"Not for ladies, eh!" He wagged a finger.

Disobedient to the core, I turned back and joined them. They were crowded three deep around a fresco in the porter's lodge. I burrowed my way under Gerald's arm and in the dim light saw the fresco of a man weighing his colossal organ on a pair of scales.

"To ward off the Evil Eye," Bang Bang whispered, pulling on his lower eyelid. A Sheela-na-Gig, Italian Style. Northern climes embraced the power of the female while warmer ones that of the male. Was it to do with the difference between a pastoral and a nomadic culture? Had women more power where the soil was tilled? I always knew there was a good reason to grow your own vegetables.

Bang Bang was horrified to see me.

"*Sposata?*" he asked.

"Only just," I whispered.

He put his finger to his lips and led me gently outside.

On our last evening we dined in the best restaurant in town, famous for its *spezzatino di beccaccia*, according to Gerald. Every morsel melted in the mouth like candyfloss.

"How was that?" Gerald enquired, with a slight chuckle.

"You'd prefer me to have left some on the side of my plate, just to show how well bred I am?"

"Nothing at all like that, Philippa. I merely wondered whether you knew what you'd been eating."

He had me there. I recognised the polenta chips and the gravy flavoured with rocket, the rest was immaterial.

"Casseroled woodcock." His chuckle was now a full-bodied whoop of laughter, complete with tears dripping down his sideburns. "Though I'm sure," he said, trying to mop his face and limit the damage, "the real thing would be infinitely superior."

I let him away with it, this time. A girl needs to relax after a heavy meal.

We finished the chianti as the sun set across the bay and my nipples stood to attention in the stiff breeze.

"I suppose all good things come to an end," Gerald sighed, delicately mopping the chianti on his soft lips.

"It's really supposed to be the beginning," I reminded him.

"You know what I mean. The end of the honeymoon."

I knew exactly what he meant. We were due to leave for Woodleigh Hall on the first plane from Rome in the morning. Life would never be the same again.

"Still, I suppose we could go on the odd holiday – Aran perhaps? Or Bath? Or even Paris?"

Anywhere but Paris. It held too many ghosts. The past is always present.

Around us, the sky was deepening to navy blue. A large family, cousins, sisters and aunts included, had taken a long table beneath the lanterns now splotched with suicidal moths. The Italians love children and take them everywhere. Two were asleep already, one on its grandmother's lap and the other across the table, bottom in the air, its chubby hands cradling its head.

"A peaceful sight," Gerald said, smiling towards the visions of contentment. "Do I detect the maternal juices flowing?"

"Just slightly," I confessed.

"I suppose we should make a life for ourselves first before we introduce anyone else into it."

I put a half eaten truffle back on my plate and folded my arms against the chilly evening air . . .

❦ *Chapter Two* ❧

Woodleigh Hall, ancestral home of the Ransomes, reposed on the only hillock for miles. Like sagging breasts, its bay windows spread onto the grass in front. From the end of the long driveway it had the sad, forlorn look of a jilted woman. However, it cheered up on closer inspection as several hundred panes of glass glinted and smiled in the autumn sun. An iron rail led up to a portico of Corinthian columns. The apex of the pediment encased a tiny, stained glass roundel above.

"Most unusual, Gerald."

"I know I'm different . . . Oh, you mean the house."

"One of these days!" I warned. "The stained glass roundel is not a usual feature of a classical building."

"A later addition. It depicts the dove of peace. Mother had it put in after a particularly harrowing row in the porch with a gypsy. He put a curse on the doorway, said the next person to enter would be struck dead. So, she sent for the bishop and the local dowser. The bishop muttered something in Latin and the dowser threw some crystals and tested for negative vibes. The roundel was mother's own contribution. She was a great believer in the curative powers of art. Had us all painting madly away as young'uns. So, she felt this offering to the dove of peace would do the trick."

"And did it?"

"Seems to have. No one's ever died on the actual doorstep – yet."

"Better not carry me over it, in that case."

I could just see the headline *Death on the doorstep. Husband held for questioning.*

"Was she an artist, your mother?"

"Sculptress more. You'll see some of her work in the house. Takes a bit of getting used to."

We got out of the car and headed for the door. Over the side of the handrail, dug into the earth were the cellar windows, festooned with rampant creeper and ivy. Here and there a stray buddleia had found a niche and was stretching gloriously upwards. A thick layer of leaves covered the bottom.

"Slightly unkempt, I'm afraid," Gerald said. As he put the key into the lock, the door suddenly opened. Pimmsy appeared, clad in a purple smoking jacket patterned with stains in various stages of biological degradation.

"Welcome, welcome," he said, pulling back the door. "How was old Red Socks?"

"We didn't actually get an audience with him, Father. Seems the old chap is a bit busy these days."

"Never mind. Better luck next time."

"If we'd known you were so anxious we'd have asked for one of his special blessings for you," I said.

He ignored me. No sense of humour.

"Sherry, Mrs Gerald?"

"'Philippa' will do fine. Yes, a sherry would be lovely."

No sense in letting Pimmsy have all the fun.

He led us into the hallway, past a faded velvet curtain, which was designed to keep out draughts but caught dirt instead. A cat stared at us for a few seconds and then scampered up the stairs.

"That's my latest jealous familiar. She doesn't like competition," said Gerald squeezing my hand.

"Reassure her I'm happy to share you. I think you'll be well able for two felines."

As we were about to go through the opened door, I saw a shadow pass the end of the hall and disappear into the blackness. I suddenly felt cold and pulled my coat tighter around me.

Pimmsy beckoned me into a sitting-room large enough to accommodate several small bungalows or drill a company of soldiers. A red Persian carpet with a faded tree of life pattern went from one end to the other, its frayed edges spilling onto the wooden surrounds.

"Well, good health and long years of whatever and all that," Pimmsy said handing us each a grubby crystal glass. "Don't stand on ceremony, have a seat."

There were two couches and several armchairs, all falling apart. I couldn't decide which one might have a vestige of a spring, so I let Gerald choose. He picked a blue, silk-covered two-seater with faded tapestry cushions exposing their innards. However, it was mercifully close to the fire. The marble mantelpiece was carried on the shoulders of two putti whose cheeks were blackened by smoke.

"Father, you could have cut the wood!" Gerald exclaimed.

Resting on the fender was a four foot length of wood whose burning tip was deep in the grate.

"Uses the same principle as a burning cigarette," Pimmsy said, pushing the tree trunk forward another inch.

"And just as smoky," said Gerald coughing.

Pimmsy cleared his throat loudly and left the room.

"Slightly sensitive is old Pater," Gerald sighed.

Selfish old devil, if you were to ask me. But people seldom do. They don't like the truth.

"Well, it is smoky, even the putti's blushes are black."

"At least we're on our own now." An arm disappeared round my back and popped up at my front. "It might be interesting to see what colour *your* blushes are in a dark, smoky room."

We did what all newly married couples generally do before boredom and the chill of winter set in.

Something flashed at the window as I paused to get my bearings.

"Gerald! What was that?," I said pointing to the blackness outside.

"Probably Buggerlugs skulking around, dropping around the eves."

"Who?"

"My charming brother, Mortimer."

"The same one who didn't bother to turn up to our wedding?"

"The same, though I can't say I missed his brooding presence. Indulged by Mother until he thought adulation was nothing more than his due. Unfortunately the rest of the world never found him as wonderful as she did. Quite the opposite."

"You never talk about him."

"I try to put him out of my mind. I keep hoping he'll disappear into a vat of slurry or fall off that damned horse of his."

"Any more surprises in store?"

"Lots!" he said leaning towards me. "I'm really a red hot rapist *chez moi*. I lured you here so I could make mad passionate love at my every whim." He clutched me even tighter. "The entire estate is surrounded by a moat that's packed to the gills with

English crocodiles, specially bred to withstand ten degrees of frost and a delicacy in their own right."

"Try pulling the other one," I said, hopefully. "Bet you haven't a clue what a croc tastes like."

"Of course I have – like a strongly flavoured prawn. *Croc au vin* is a Woodleigh Hall special. This is how you grab 'em."

"Gerald!"

I won't go into the details of the next hour or so, except that the shadows on the walls made very interesting shapes and the fire crackled and roared its background music.

In the cold light of day, the interior of Woodleigh Hall had the sort of *gravitas* one sees in a Renaissance fresco, although faded and flaking. A great house definitely down at heel, forming not only midnight but daytime feasts for woodworm. Polish on the oak panelling or curved banisters was a distant memory. In the dining-room the pattern vied for ascendancy with the mildew on the yellow silk wallpaper as flower-filled urns shed more petals than were realistically possible. The persian carpet was threadbare. The ubiquitous Primavera scene, shorn of its flowers and finery now boasted only shadows and hints of former beauty.

There were two fireplaces, one near the table so the diners didn't freeze to death while eating their partridge *à l'ancienne*, and the other so that they

could relax and enjoy their port in relative comfort.
The tables and balloon-backed chairs ached for
nourishment. A dozen tins of beeswax wouldn't
even touch the surface.

An ebonised cabinet filled the long gap between
the fireplaces, though the brown film of dirt on the
glass made it difficult to see whether it contained
the genuine article or Czechoslovakian copies. In
the pervading gloom of the room, without fires or
sunlight to cheer it, it was difficult to imagine
happy dinner parties or jolly get-togethers. I
wondered whether the table had ever borne a feast,
heard the tinkle of glasses or seen the glorious
softness of candlelight on young faces. And I
wondered too whether my children would ever sit
there and eat baked beans on toast or sing *Happy
Birthday*.

The rest of the house went from the shabbiness
of neglect to the discomfort of decay. Coldness
pervaded the gloom of bedrooms whose windows
were tightly shuttered against either light or
darkness. In the spare room a climbing ivy
stretched towards a chink of light, its root
embedded in a deerstalker.

"Below stairs" bore testimony to a past which
could afford a bevy of housemaids. The boot room
had rows of pegs on which to hang polished boots
for the coming hunt or to dry those dampened by a
November downpour. And of course the dairy, with

its flagstone floor and tiny window to keep out the heat and keep in the cool, was witness to the fact that the house had once been self-sufficient in butter and cheese.

Our bedroom was a disgrace. Designed to put one off all forms of sensuality. The tomb-like coldness allowed for little freedom of expression while the distempered walls with their patterns of cracks and mould didn't encourage one to linger.

"Close your eyes to it all," Gerald said.

"I like to have my eyes open, Gerald," I explained. "And when I look at the room I see nothing but death and decay. I wonder who was here last, who was it who enjoyed the same bed and are now no more. Who was it who painted that faded flower on the window glass, a lone camomile. Waiting."

"You sound almost poetic at times, Pips. Ever think of writing?"

"I don't know the first thing about poetry."

"Best way to go about it. Nothing kills inspiration quicker than a classical education. You become intimidated by the past instead of embracing the now."

I thought it was a crazy suggestion at the time. But Gerald has insight. I penned a little poem and showed it to him at dinner.

Camomile window
Sunny centre; moonlike petals
Reflect love.

"A haiku!" Gerald gasped, wiping the last crumb of steak and kidney pie from his delicious lips. "I've always wanted to write one of those. Philippa, you're incredible. I feel very jealous."

"Then it must be good!"

My explorations of the house continued apace. I marvelled at the stucco ceilings, the perfect proportions of the rooms and made an inventory of the dark, dusty paintings. And, for the first time, I entered Gerald's mother's room.

Facing south, it was full of light. The centre-piece of the mullioned window depicted autumn, with trees dropping their leaves like showers of gold onto the earth beneath. As they touched the ground they became miniature works of art, depicting people carving, painting or drawing. By far the biggest room upstairs, it was dominated by a four-poster bed with carved trunk-like columns carrying a faded *Toile de Jouy* canopy. It must have taken an army of slaves to carry the bed bit by bit up the long stairs.

The spiders were having a field day, weaving their threads from the chandelier in the centre of the ceiling to the corners of the four-poster and back again. Each corner of the walls, from top to bottom, was lined with little fly-catching webs. The fireplaces at either end of the room, though not as fine as those in the rooms downstairs, were slim and elegant. The long, narrow twigs from rooks' nests choked the grates and spilled onto the hearth. I moved round the bed, trying not to make a sound or step on any of the pieces of sculpture that littered the floor. As I brought my head up, the green eyes of a snake on either side of a broad, flat head, glinted back. Like an idiot I yelled like mad and ran. Fortunately no one heard the mad Irishwoman. I tore down the long staircase and grabbed the bottle of Scotch from the cocktail cabinet to put a reviving thimbleful in my tea. I made a mental note to have the Scotch *before* I set foot in the room next time.

Of course, stupidly, I thought I was a gift to these poor people in Woodleigh Hall who had no female person to look after them – no one to wash Pimmsy's dirty shirts or take his stained smoking jacket to the cleaners.

"What do you enjoy eating?" I asked him, as I washed the grime from presses and worktops and scrubbed the pine table.

"Food, generally," was the reply, at which Mortido, *né* Mortimer, sniggered. I decided to ignore the bad manners and went womanfully on.

"Of course – but fish, beef, lamb, chicken?"

"Yes, please."

I could see I was getting places. The presence of Mortido was hugely encouraging to Pimmsy's rudeness.

I forged ahead: real vegetable soup to start with – a sort of "pavement pizza" soup with turnip, parsnip, carrot and onion sieved until unrecognisable. I always cheat by adding a packet. As a main course I decided on fish pie with potato topping. I was already missing my little farm, its freezer stocked with sun-sweetened garden peas. Not to mention my solid fuel cooker warming the kitchen and cooking a casserole to perfection.

"The Aga is useless," Pimmsy had said that first morning. After several unsuccessful attempts to light it, I agreed. Large fry-ups with black and white pudding and streaky bacon, enlivened by an omelette at the weekend, were cooked on a camping gas ring. All served on the best Minton china. Even the cat drank from a delph dish – badly cracked certainly.

"Couldn't we get the Aga fixed?" I ventured. Pimmsy and Mortido said nothing and sat staring into space, though there was some sort of movement of feet under the table.

"After all, it would make the kitchen warmer."

They were playing dead. However, Gerald agreed wholeheartedly and the service man came to scrape inches of dirt, clean the chimney and at the end of the day had it going full steam.

"Now we can have some caramel slices," I announced to my new family. Not a flicker of anticipation. Except from Gerald.

"That would be very nice, Philippa."

I really love that man.

I put the base in the oven and prepared the toffee filling. There is a fine line between creating a caramel filling and fudging it. Emily always uses a thermometer. But then she's a careful sort of person, except when it comes to choosing a husband.

"Perhaps you'd keep on eye out for what's in the oven," I said to Pimmsy as I trotted upstairs with Gerald's mug of coffee and, hopefully, his last packet of bought biscuits.

I wasn't really sure whether I really liked being married to a writer. It meant I was a word processor widow for several hours every day. When Gerald was actually typing feverishly and had an 'intent' look on his face, I was not to disturb him. If, however, he was looking out the window or caressing the cat, I was welcome to stay.

Nice to have people around who will allow you to indulge yourself.

"What if the house is on fire and you're sitting there about to have your fingers bathed in melting plastic?" I enquired.

"No need to exaggerate, Philippa. I'm sure I'll smell something burning, even if it's only my hair."

I wondered whether he deserved any of my caramel slices.

The smell of something burning assailed my

nostrils on my return to the kitchen. I opened the oven door to a cloud of smoke. The base of the caramel slices was a charred mess, except for a piece in the centre the size of a pound coin. I looked at the pot with the caramel filling. The contents were somewhat depleted, the dripping spoon sitting on the cooker top. Through the kitchen window I watched Mortido wipe his mouth on his sleeve and Pimmsy suck on a cigarette.

I threw the sucked spoon into the Aga's fiery furnace. "Hope you rot in hell, you dirty bastard!" I shouted after it, Mortido's image burning in the hot flames. I grabbed the tin with the burnt base and bashed it against the firebox, spilling its black contents onto the burning spoon. "You rotten, drunken creep!" I screamed at Pimmsy's image. The empty pot I slid along the floor, where it clattered and came to a halt at the pantry door.

Just as well they'd sneaked off – they'd live.

"Precisely what am I supposed to occupy my time with while you're busy acquiring a nervous breakdown on that keyboard, Gerald?"

Gerald looked at me as if I had just taken off all my clothes.

"Well, I *would* like to know. Am I to scrub the centuries of grime from the floors of Woodleigh Hall, take up knitting, visit the poor or cook vats of *Croc au Vin*? You did mention something about the walled garden and summers of strawberries with cream."

"And now is just about the time to get them in. Thought these might be a help," he said, placing a selection of the finest steel garden tools at my feet.

"How kind of you," I managed to say while noticing with dismay that they were all made for the Little Lady and therefore half the size of a decent set.

Obediently, I made my way to the walled garden. It had become overgrown and utterly useless. Whatever fruit bushes there had been were now spindly, fighting for light through the weeds. Espalier pears were a discredit to their name; the plums and greengages could have done with a good feed.

I had cleared one and a half pathways when my doings obviously got too much for the biscuit burners and it was time to bring in the cavalry. Big Sis, Sybil Sheepshanks arrived with her sickly child and silent husband.

"We don't require the walled garden to be put into production," she informed me. "It's far cheaper to buy vegetables and fruit than it is to grow 'em yourself," she boomed, as I tugged a bramble from its moorings.

"Is that so?" I replied. I lifted the sickle and with an enormous, show-off sort of swipe, I deheaded the thistles beneath a very elegant John Downey.

"It *is* so," she emphasised, her lips swelling around her buck teeth. "I find it difficult to talk to people when they won't look at me," she persisted.

"Really? Must be a dreadful handicap."

I react quite badly to people telling me what to do, especially when they are as sour as Mrs Mutton.

Mortido skulked through the gate and sidled up to support his next of kin. Of course, he didn't say a word. He let everyone else fight his battles for him.

"And Mortimer likes to have the walled garden free to rear his pheasants in and, as I'm sure even *you* are aware, the chicks must not be disturbed."

"In that case," I suggested in my most reasonable tone, "why not put them in the disused building at the edge of the lake. They would have access to water and be completely undisturbed. Growing vegetables will play havoc with their weight gain, particularly when I bring in the rotovator."

This really wasn't the answer they expected. While I continued chopping and clearing, they stood apart. Sybil whispered for all she was worth into the face of her husband who reminded me of the Polled Dorset ram PJ bought one year only to discover he had come without anything in his "pouch". *Spongy balls* was how PJ put it. "No sense in having a ram with a gun and no bullets!" he'd said. Mr Sheepshanks had at least one bullet in his gun at some time – unless their offspring was engendered by AI. Obviously a poor straw.

The whispering stopped. Merely *reculer pour mieux sauter*. Sheepshanks now squared her rounded shoulders and thrust her over-large *enbonpoint* in my direction, followed by her shuffling entourage.

I smiled. Always dismay the enemy.

"You're nothing but a jumped-up, stinking, Irish pig!"

"Lovely animals, pigs. They know how to keep their shit to one side, unlike some I could mention but I'm far too polite to name names," I replied, keeping the smile plastered on my face as best I could, though war is never pleasant.

"You listen here to me! You caught our dear brother in a weak moment. Nothing but a gold digging Irish clodhopper! If you think a Papist will ever run Woodleigh, then think again!"

The bit about Gerald stung momentarily. Perhaps he didn't love me after all; perhaps it was all a giant mistake.

When I raised my head again to say something equally devastating, Mrs Mutton & Co had disappeared like snow off a ditch.

They stayed to dinner. I casseroled the rabbit Gerald got from one of his pet gamekeepers. It nestled amongst onions, carrots, turnip and courgette.

"Rabbit!" Madame Mutton shrieked like a

banshee. "Vermin!" she said pulling her plate from beneath Gerald's ladleful. "Do you also eat rats and mice in that country of yours?" she asked me.

"Oh, anything we can lay our hands on. I knew someone who even fried his pet goldfish – it is carp after all," I lied. Mr Mutton gobbled his helping before the rest of us had been served or the grace said.

"Try a glass of wine, Philippa," Gerald suggested, placing a restraining hand on my leg. "Goes very well with rabbit, made specially for it, I believe," he said to the assembled heap of miserable humanity.

However, Big Sis "only" drank whiskey. Wine probably took too long to have any effect. Her husband stretched sheepishly towards the proffered bottle. Big Sis pretended she wasn't bothered but you could smell the smoke billowing from her. Or perhaps I'd had too much wine. The Skulk drank his milk. Far be it from him to be cheerful company, or indeed, any sort of company.

Gerald and Mr Mutton finished the casserole between them. Mr Mutton sucked the bones dry and laid them side by side on his plate in quite a fetching pattern. Their little lamb played with a mushroom and ate me with her eyes.

Old Pimmsy had the right idea and disappeared for the evening to "chat to the tenantry". Probably ensconced in the old lodge sipping his Pimms and smoking his lungs out.

"A morgue would be a more cheerful place," I said to Gerald when they'd gone to their respective hidey holes. "There's some huge anomaly here. Were they adopted – or were you? They seem to have a monopoly on the least charming aspects of the Ransome family."

"Yes. Not the sort of people you would want to have at a party. If they weren't related, you wouldn't want to know them."

Surprised by his candour, I pressed on.

"They had the cheek to criticise what I was doing in the garden." I spared him a blow by blow account. "I felt like chopping their heads into tiny pieces but chopped some thistle heads instead."

"Really, Philippa, you have some blood-curdling expressions. Must be the Celtic blood in you."

The poor man thought I was joking.

✿ Chapter Three ✿

One wet afternoon, when I was busy trying to find a mouse to give it its last supper, the vicar called.

"We'd heard that the young Lord of the Manor had taken unto himself a wife but we had not set eyes on her. I came to see whether there was flesh to the rumour."

A small man with a stiff neck – a sign of rigidity. Surely not in a Church of England pastor? Perhaps he was one of those who was against the ordination of women.

"How do you do, Reverend – or is it Mr?"

His neck stiffened even more. Perhaps he realised I was not "one of them".

"Canon actually – Goodhew. But don't bother. Call me Simon."

"Well . . . Simon. Won't you have tea?"

Both tea and coffee were refused. I had a blinding flash of the obvious and poured a glass of whisky.

"Cheers," we said to each other – me with a smallish sherry, just to be sociable.

An hour later the whisky and sherry bottle were looking decidedly off-peak. I opened another. A Scottish malt and a very pleasant-tasting oloroso.

"You have kept the good wine till the last, Philly."

"Aren't we worth it, Simey? What better way to spend a wet afternoon than chatting to someone who really understands you, likes the same sort of music and loves nature. The only difference is that for you there's a big daddy in the sky looking after it all."

"That sounds a trifle blasphemous, Philly. God does exist, you know. And if he didn't, we would have invented him."

I'd heard that little nugget about a million years ago but I let it pass. I wanted to hear a bit more about Mrs Simon.

"Wonderful with the poor. Tremendous heart. Puts me to shame sometimes. You see, I can't help noticing the smell of the poor, their snotty noses, bad teeth. Gladys seems to see beyond all that, like Mother Teresa. It's a gift, a gift."

"You really think it's a gift and not a habit?"

"Definitely. Of course, poor sight is a help and Gladys would tell you herself that she lost her sense of smell years ago. Can't even smell a sprig of lavender if you shove it up her hooter! Oops, I'm getting a bit giddy. But it's so nice to relax, isn't it, Philly. They say such dreadful things about Papists but I must say, you seem a bit of all right."

The vote of confidence cheered me up no end.

"We're all the same under the skin, I think," I said with the merest hint of a slur, and filled the glasses once again. Nothing so forlorn as an empty glass with finger marks around the edge signalling the end of the party.

"Give or take," Simey said, roaring with laughter. "Speaking of which, how are all the Ransomes – the old man being hospitable?"

"His first love is Mrs Pimms, after that he's not bothered except for getting a square meal a day. Ate his way through some leftover rabbit the other night, though his daughter turned up her nose at it."

"I'll let you in on a little secret – they say she's a third son in drag!"

I knew what he meant, the lack of feminine charm.

"You don't say . . . ," I encouraged.

"Well, there was talk of unladylike – or perhaps too ladylike – behaviour. No, no more whiskey. Already eating into my Christmas ration. Gladys can't stand the smell of it on a man's breath."

"I thought she'd no sense of smell?"

"That's exactly what I said to her the last time and she replied that you'd want to be pretty far gone not to smell something as strong as whisky."

There are none so holy as those who will not smell. Gladys seemed quite a handful.

"You must bring Mrs Canon with you on your next visit – to see the garden. Perhaps she'd like some flowers for the church."

He got unsteadily to his feet and clasped both my hands in his.

"How very kind of you, Pips. I'll tell her that directly. And what a wonderful person you are, so charitable and generous."

For a horrible moment I thought he was going to kiss me; but it was just that his head was getting too heavy to carry and it sort of flopped forward. We went arm in arm to his car. I hoped Big Daddy would look after his own. He eased himself behind the steering wheel and pulled the wings of his head-rest to support his jaws. Head up he sailed down the driveway, scaring a pheasant half to death and slightly altering the contour of the grass verge.

Gerald was in a really bad mood when he finally descended hours later.

"Philippa! Who's been at the oloroso?"

I smiled my most alluring in the hope of diverting his attention. But Gerald is one of those who is focused, a sticker. Unfortunately.

"I've had a nit's knapsackful to be neighbourly with the Vicar. Thought I was doing you a favour, after all he's nothing to me."

"And the whisky! Do you realise that Vicars are used to Communion wine and wouldn't know a single malt if it jumped up and bit them. What a waste!"

"He enjoyed every minute of it. Here's me trying to do my level best for you socially and all you can do is complain. Really Gerald, if this is marriage, then I'd rather pack it all in and go back to my little farm."

I hated using blackmail but sometimes a girl can be driven to extremes.

"Before you do that, replace that bottle of malt!" he said and stormed from the room.

Blackmail doesn't seem to work with Gerald.

Mrs Simey lost no time in taking up her invitation. She appeared on the portico the following morning. Her grey shape was at one with the dull, drizzly day.

"Well, it's very nice of you to visit so soon," I lied through my teeth.

She gave me one of those appraising looks, the sort Lady Bracknell reserved for prospective sons-in-law.

"Simon was in rather a sinful state when he came home."

I wanted to say I didn't put a gun or indeed anything to his head to force malt down his throat. I smiled instead.

"Well, won't you come in?" She brushed past me into the hallway.

Obviously no stranger to the house, she stalked her way to the sitting-room.

"A glass of something to warm you up?" Perhaps she'd come for her share of the malt.

"Certainly not! I am strictly TT. The stuff has never passed my lips."

I felt like waxing lyrical on the delights of imbibing just to cheer myself up but I held back. There was something like horror behind her words.

"Oh, really?" I encouraged.

"The curse of the peasantry. Cause of laziness and unwanted children."

Perhaps old Simey made an advance last night in his malty mood.

"I didn't think the peasantry could afford enough bread, let alone intoxicating liquors."

"They will forego clothes, food and even plate money for the stuff."

Now, that was serious. No din-dins for Canon Goodhew and wife.

Her face screwed itself up into a tight ball with a brisk contraction of muscles that must have taken years to train, and then relaxed. Exhausting to watch.

"Won't you sit down," I said almost fainting. "Perhaps a cup of tea, coffee?"

"Coffee would be nice."

I plugged in the percolator.

"I see you're well organised," Mrs Simey said.

"It takes at least half a day to get to the kitchen from here. In an old house, one must be resourceful."

"I couldn't agree more. Spend, spend, spend is all people can think of nowadays while the hedgerows rot with unpicked berries: rose hips full of vitamin C, and blackberries. You could feed a child from the hedges alone."

"Well, I don't actually agree with shooting birds or robbing their nests for eggs. Four and twenty blackbirds baked in a pie would not appeal."

"You would eat anything if you're hungry enough."

There was no arguing with that but I was damned if I was going to agree with her. We exchanged recipes while I poured the coffee.

"Now to business," she said, having finished the packet of bourbon biscuits and the last of the coffee. Waste not want not.

"Simon tells me you were discussing important parish business and how you might help the poor. We have a whist drive once a month and a jumble sale. Old clothes, baking and unwanted gifts are most acceptable. The jumble sale is next Friday. We're taking deliveries at the Rectory."

She put down her cup, screwed her face into a semblance of a smile and made for the door.

"My regards to Gerald. Lucky woman to have taken such a prize."

I detected a distinct whiff of begrudgery.

Her driving was not nearly as interesting as her husband's. She drove the same way she lived: on the straight and narrow.

The days that followed were full of that stiff politeness only a lover's tiff can bestow. And when the anger subsided, there was the ache to chat, if only to remark on the flight of a bird or the height to which a sponge had risen. Pride forbids us to be the first to speak. However, on the fourth day, I compromised and replaced the bottle of malt. A bunch of freesias appeared on my plate at dinner time and I bestowed a smile.

"Missed you," Gerald whispered out of earshot of Pimmsy and Mortido. "Silly to get so worked up by a bottle of malt. Probably jealousy. I grudge anyone time spent with you, when I could be enjoying your company."

I was about to say "Put a boot through your PC screen, just to show willing" when I noticed the threads of moisture at the corners of his eyes and of course I melted. Married life wasn't too bad after all. Just a shame it depends so much on the other person.

Old Pimmsy and the Skulk ate with us – the latter slobbering down whatever was before him and the former weighing up how much it was safe to eat without mopping up the alcohol in his bloodstream. Fortunately, as soon as the food was finished, they both disappeared to their respective lairs. Gerald and I then poured the port and I put out the cheese I'd been hiding.

"Delicious din-dins, Philippa. Irish Stew?"

"The genuine article. There are so many imitations. It must have mutton, not beef; potato and onion only. Carrots are a travesty."

"You're so knowledgeable, Pippy. I was thinking, all alone with my word processor, not able to write a thing for three days," he said, popping a chunk of cheese into his mouth, "how perhaps you're not being sufficiently 'stretched' – if you'll pardon the expression – here at Woodleigh."

I was so pleased to hear he suffered on my account – not that I wished him any harm . . .

"Well, the garden is taking a lot of my time," I said, pouring the merest hint of brandy into the coffee. "I want it to be 'organic', so I've to weed it by hand and foot. The soil then needs to be covered with a green manure to give the bugs some food. All the fruit bushes have been given the scrapings from the sheephouse, in convenient little pellets. The more I see of sheep, the more I admire them."

"Perhaps you could put some of your ideas into action, Pips. I know Mortimer does the day-to-day work but perhaps he could do with some direction. The farm needs to make more money. That's why the old man wanted me back here. He doesn't realise writing just about saps any creative juice. But I know, darling, you have more than enough for both of us."

"Give me free reign and I'll do my worst – I mean my best." I winked. Though working with the Skulk was not my idea of fun.

"The other thing is . . ." I toyed with the crumbs on my plate. "I would like to do a little re-organising in the bedroom, get the chimney swept so that we can have some heat. I imagine winter at Woodleigh could be quite trying."

"Of course, you do as you wish to make yourself comfortable. That was the condition under which I came back here. Living in tatty gentility never appealed to me." He stretched out a hand for mine and squeezed.

I could not have heard sweeter words. I already had the colour scheme planned. Restrained yet cheerful. Elegant yet comfortable.

The dark brown and red imitation William Morris paper was steamed off in a few hours by the Aga service man. The plaster beneath was surprisingly good. I changed my mind about more wallpaper and decided to paint instead. White with the merest blush to it. Mr Aga was doubtful.

"Get dirty" was his worry. Unlikely in a house with several spare rooms for grubby hands to do their worst. Between us, we had it painted before the week was out.

"It's brighter, more . . . spiritual looking," Gerald said.

Exactly.

The following week I had the muslin curtains up and my trousseau of lace-bordered bed linen in place. Coir matting gave a final air of simple sophistication with the Bokaras freshly shampooed and artfully scattered. Mr Aga cleaned the limed oak bookcase and replaced the torn and mildewed fabric on its shelves with bright yellow silk. We lit the fire.

"My, my," he whispered, "In't something. Some folks is very lucky."

"That depends on the heart within – *Better a dinner of herbs where love is, than a stalled ox and hatred therewith:* Proverbs 24. Nothing is much use if there isn't love. All the riches on earth can't buy it."

He looked at me as if I'd flipped my lid.

"Don't know 'bout that. You could alus be miserable in luxury."

I let him have the last word, just to cheer him up.

The huge fire heated the room to the temperature of spring in Menton and cast a glow everywhere. I spent longer than usual at the dressing table preparing for dinner. Gerald brought some seasoned logs from a fallen apple tree; their scent filled the air. In the firelight he looked, not exactly a clichéd "rugged" but certainly handsome, male, infinitely desirable.

"Can I get you anything else, Pips?" he asked.

I didn't dare say what was on my mind, thoughts unbefitting a lady, to do with crisp linen sheets, lace and a well-sprung mattress. I was supposed to be a respectable married woman with household chores, gardening and farming on her mind.

"You seem sad, Pippy. Anything I can do? Aren't you happy with your creation?"

My husband doesn't understand me.

"Perhaps you need a rest before dinner. Here, let me take those shoes off. Put your feet up."

I never knew whether he read my mind or was a total innocent but the evening passed in the most glorious imaginable communion with flesh and soul. His very odour was enough to cause me to reel in ecstasy, just as Pavlov's dogs eventually salivated at the sound of a bell. All wrong for an old married couple.

Dinner was later than usual. Nothing had spoilt but rather improved with the long, slow cooking. Just like the build-up to an orgasm.

"Beef olives – my favourite. Pips, you're a wonder."

Did he ever doubt it?

◖ *Chapter Four* ◗

"Bet you thought they'd all forgotten you at home," Gerald said, handing me a letter across the toast and marmalade.

I only wished they had. Andy's writing; there must be something wrong.

Dear Sis

How's that old Bruce of yours then, eh? Bet you're spoiling him rotten, lucky devil. Could do with a bit of decent grub meself. Glorry has this love affair with chick peas and lentils, they pop up everywhere, even in ice cream.

Having a poor do with the porkies. They keep rooting for buried treasure or something. When one of 'em finds an old root its squeal brings the whole lot for a snout-wrestle. Pretty tiring to watch. Glorry says all this sort of thing is displacement behaviour and they're desperate for sex. She says we should put them out of their misery. Know any bores?

Love,
BRO

"Try the archaeological society," I mumbled.

"Did you say something, Pippy?"

"Nothing important. Just that my brother still can't spell. Gerald, things don't look good at home."

"Someone dead?"

"Not yet. Barely a snout away."

"Pigs?"

"Ghoulish Gloria is on the rampage again. Why did I ever think I could leave a stuffed pike with her, let alone a farm full of animals?"

"Now come and sit down."

"I thought Andy had a bit of sense but he seems like a limp willy, allowing all this madness free expression."

The phone rang.

Andy.

"Just to say if you got the letter, tear it up. Discovered what was ailing the pigs. Glorry had run out of food and didn't bother getting more. Poor buggers were half starved, digging for Australia, looking for grub."

"This is ridiculous, Andrew. Are you not keeping an eye on things? After all, Glorry is not a blood relation."

"Don't go on about all that again! She's a great character, just off-beam at times. Bit like yourself."

I put the phone down as gently as the circumstances allowed.

I penned a quick note to Emily.

Dear Em

Worried sick about animals – any chance you could "happen to be passing" and take a quick look – just to make sure everyone (i.e. four footed) is alive and well? Surreptitiously.

Married bliss is just that . . . Woodleigh is quite a handful. Don't think I've seen all the rooms yet. Garden's coming along. Hope archaeological soc are well – regards to all.

Love
Philippa

I decided to post it immediately, and searched out my wax jacket and wellies. Woodleigh Village is typically English: restrained, civilised and tidy. Houses with tiny windows peep out from a canopy of thatch. When the light is just right, you can glimpse the ubiquitous designer beams, huge open fires, upholstered fenders and Clarice Cliff plates gathering dust on whitewashed walls. The sort of places where you never see any washing on the line or dustbins spilling their contents to the delight of little brown dogs. People in Woodleigh live out of Marks & Spencer bags and sip mulled wine to the sounds of Mendelssohn. Gerald says they're all yuppies or dinkies.

"So?" I said to him. "There are worse things."

"I doubt it," he replied. "Their pleasures come from *telling* you about the exciting things they've done – and therefore you *ought* to do. Rarely do they experience anything for itself."

"Perhaps that's a good thing. Wouldn't do if folks were 'experiencing' all over the place. No pleasure left in watching their repression strategies – the tight lips, stiff necks and rigid bottoms."

"Really, Philippa. You have the capacity to shock me from time to time."

He held my arm as I pulled on my boots.

"Me? Mild as a dove!"

"That wouldn't be the sort of bird I was thinking of."

"Do you ever let up, Gerald, and play truant for a day or so? Does being a writer mean you're a slave to your word processor?"

"Yes."

A master of restraint, just when you want something more.

"You never told me about this, Gerald." I fastened the studs on my Barbour. "I thought I was marrying a twin soul, a cushion for my fears and disappointments, someone to share this miserable hour we have upon the stage before the lights go out."

"Really?"

Sometimes I could kill him.

"Didn't you want companionship? Scintillating

conversation? A safe port when the storms of the world have tossed you about?

"Not just now!"

"So why on earth did you marry me and cart me to this mausoleum with a crazy sister, a drunken father and a creep for a brother?"

"Because I love you." He opened the door for me. "Aren't you going to say goodbye?" he asked.

My proffered lips were met with an urgency that almost took my breath away.

"Can't the post wait?" he whispered.

I allowed myself to be led upstairs, hoping my thumping heart didn't betray my eagerness. Before I'd finished undoing my coat studs, Gerald had a nest of pillows and duvet on the floor.

"Save you taking off your boots," he said, considerate as always.

We made mad, passionate love – at least I did; I was too busy to notice what Gerald was doing.

The post office is a tiny single-storey building in the middle of the village. Everything wooden is painted red, this being England. Even the postmistress is red-faced, twenty letters a day to stamp and she's out of puff. Still unmarried, Constance Bates was left at the altar by a traveller in thread about twenty years ago. Gerald says he was a horror anyway and she was well out of it. I have my suspicions that old Mrs Bates had something to do with it. She sits beside the door, letting the last of the autumn sunshine bounce off her leathery skin.

"Good day, Mrs Ransome. Nice weather for the time of year."

"Aren't we after being the lucky ones, Mrs B? No rain for at least an hour."

"You're used to rain in Southern Ireland, of course."

"The rain falls everywhere, Mrs Bates, North and South alike. We're all under one sky."

This was news to her. She closed her wrinkled eyelids slowly, like a tortoise.

"Ah, but it's the local influences what counts."

She had me there.

A small white dog came nosing along and cocked his leg at her chair. The wet trickled down and met her shoe.

"I see what you mean," I bent conspiratorially towards her. "Sit around and you get urinated upon."

In the worst possible taste, but I couldn't resist it.

Gladys Goodhew pulled up to give me a lift just as I was on my way home and admiring the sun sinking behind the oak trees on the edge of Woodleigh estate. Though all the other trees had lost most of their leaves in the frost and wind, the oaks still retained their crowning glory and swayed in the evening breeze.

"Just coming to visit you, Mrs Ransome."

I obediently got into the car and searched in vain for the seat belt.

"Sorry, it's not there any longer. Used in a splint for a parishioner's leg."

"A novel idea the manufacturer's probably never thought of."

"One must be practical."

We leapt forward as she made a quick gear change. I braced my knees against the dashboard.

"Speaking of which," she went on, "I was coming to invite you to the parish council meeting tonight – that is if your husband can spare you. I know you would like to get involved with the poor and help them to a better future. You're a woman after my own heart. The Canon says the same."

How could he, the traitor! I hope I was as unlike Gladys as a goat from a rabbit. Perhaps such flattery got him a better dinner – or something . . .

"What does it involve, Gladys?"

"What it means is that we tell the poor and the lazy how to improve their lot, how to become self-sufficient, so that on the Day of Judgment they can say they did their very best."

Sounded fun.

"Pick you up at eight. Bring a coat, it can be cold in the parish hall."

Gladys spoke not a word of a lie. Under the stars would have been warmer. Draughts streamed in everywhere they could, particularly through the gap in the floorboards. It smelt of dead mice and dust. A few plates of sandwiches hunched under cling film. At least there would be a cup of tea.

"How is Philippa?"

The Canon looked resplendent in black jacket, black silk blouse and twinkling eyes. Not bad looking, in a roguish sort of way.

"Wonderful, O Big Gun." He laughed at my feeble joke, a real gentleman. "And your good self?" I enquired.

"Looking forward to a hot cup of tea and some of Glad's sambos – they're the only ones that won't have salmonella, which I'm a little averse to. I've enough running to do in my job!"

A small circle was gathering beside us. Looking.

"And," he said, gesturing to an inside pocket, "I've a little something to take the heat out of the tea."

A silver pilgrim bottle with an incised pattern glinted at me.

"Canon! The St Bernard of Woodleigh Village."

It was his turn to giggle. A few necks went stiffer and ears flapped.

"All in the line of duty. 'Whan that Aprille with his shoures sote' folks go on pilgrimage'. Wouldn't do if vicar caught a chill on the way to Canterbury. You're coming with us in spring, I hope?"

"A pilgrimage? To Canterbury? Of course!"

We both giggled. That did it. Gladys banged the kettle with some sort of blunt instrument. Probably her head.

"We tend to be timeous here," she said – in reference to my Irish casualness, no doubt.

The flapping ears relaxed, as chairs were scraped and papers shuffled. Gladys looked at each person in turn.

"Now, the business of the meeting is to get everyone who is fit and able-bodied to help those less fortunate. We need jobs. There are fifty people on t'dole in Woodleigh, in a village where Mrs Jenkins here can't find anyone to do a bit of painting or gutter cleaning."

I wasn't surprised. Her face would frighten the devil off a ladder.

"We need to encourage all these . . . folks to stir theirselves a bit more," she said, breathless with missionary zeal. "They need to be shown that there is a joy in work."

"The only joy in work, Gladys, is when you stop!" Out it came before I could stop myself. Evil thrives when good women do nothing.

The vicar bent his head and caressed his pilgrim flask. Some coughed and others changed legs.

Gladys was nonplussed. "That's as may be,

Philippa, but then you probably work harder than most."

Perhaps old Glad would like my velvet-lined beaver coat to stave off the winter chill.

"What I propose is . . . " an agricultural-looking gentleman rasped.

"Yes, Mr Manifold, I'm sure we would all be happy to listen."

With the help of an ash pole, he heaved himself up and addressed the rest of us mortals.

"What comes to my mind is waste. Waste is everywhere you look. Never waste when I were a lad. Every scrap of brown paper and string were kept. Jam jars were cleaned and put away for home-made jam. My mother used to make the best strawberry jam of anyone – you remember that, Mrs Goodhew. Won all the prizes in the Woodleigh Show and a few more besides." He pulled a length of cloth from his pocket and blew into it. "All the best folks seem to be worm food now. And there's another thing, instead of throwing out the peelin's and scrapin's and green tatters, they could be fed to worms. And worms produce compost – so there's a good idea. We have everyone with a worm bin and they pool all their worm compost and Abel here modifies his little packing shed to help us pack it, and we're off. Jobs and money from waste. The worm is too much maligned. He may eat through our nearest and dearest but he's only doing what a worm does naturally . . . "

"Indeed, indeed Mr Manifold," Gladys rushed in to cool his ardour. "I've no doubt you have a point about waste. I deplore it. Only the other day I said to the Canon as he pushed half his dinner to one side of the plate 'You'll follow a crow for that one day', but I can see it may well be a – wriggle of worms?"

She laughed at her own little joke. The Canon was now clutching his pilgrim flask like a talisman.

"It's no laughing matter, Mrs Canon. It's the coming thing."

"I never for a moment thought it was the least bit funny, Mr Manifold. As usual you have some unique ideas to put forward."

With even greater care than he used to get up, Mr Manifold began the slow process of sitting down. He placed his ashplant in front and leaning on it spread his legs, gingerly edging his large bum onto the chair. The strain on his trouser seam must have been at least twenty stone to the inch and rising. For a horrible minute I thought the seam was going to split. With a shudder he landed safely. Out of such worries arise the tensions of meetings.

"Perhaps we could give someone else an opportunity to put forward their ideas," Gladys cast her eyes around the motley crew.

The rest of the evening was peppered with numerous "They should's" and "ought to's". Everyone got high on castigating the lazy crew "out there" and felt virtuous and hard-working. Tea didn't come a moment too soon. The Canon undid the chained top of his flask and poured a tot into my steaming cup with practised ease.

"That'll warm the cockles of your heart," he said with a wink.

"Where on earth did you learn such an Irish expression?"

"Sure wasn't my mother 'Oirish' and didn't I go to Trinity College."

"You don't say! We must have a chat about that."

"Long before your time, my dear. You were probably in nappies when I was learning how to drink black porter and eat crubeens."

"I was never in nappies, Canon. I was born knowing everything."

"Do you know, that's exactly what Glad said last night! 'That girl knows it all' she said just as the news was coming on the TV."

"I hate to be so transparent." Especially to Gladys.

"But you're not, Philippa. Gladys is too simple to appreciate your complications."

I didn't particularly like the way he looked at me. So I looked at the floor. A dark stain was spreading around the Canon's shoes. Not over-excitement surely in a cold, dusty hall? Probably prostate trouble. He followed my gaze.

"Good heavens above! I've forgotten to screw the top back on the flask!"

"Where on earth were you until this time of night?" Gerald asked on my return.

"Doing important parish work as befits the wife of the heir to the Woodleigh Estate. You have your duties to mankind you know, since you are privileged to own a large chunk of the planet."

"Parish work doesn't go on until two in the morning!"

"How little you appreciate what happens around you, Gerald. Locked from one end of the day to another in your ivory tower you cannot possibly understand what the rest of the world gets up to."

"Where were you?"

There was no drawing him away from his objective.

"I thought we had been through all that. If you choose not to believe me, there is nothing I can do except go to bed."

"Philippa!" he shouted at my retreating back.

If he had known the Canon and I had refilled the pilgrim flask and had gone to Woodleigh Common to watch the heavens and praise their wonders, he might not understand. I wasn't sure I understood it myself.

"Philly," the Canon said gazing up at the Milky Way. "What's all this for? What's it about?"

"What on earth do they teach you in Theological College, Simey?" I asked.

"You learn all about the history of Christianity, about the Bible, about how right the Anglican Church is and how wrong the Roman Catholic."

"Sounds highly useful," I said.

"About as useful as a bent fart, if you'll pardon my vulgarity."

"I'm a papist. It's OK to be vulgar with me."

"I knew you'd understand. Glad never does. She tells me to 'pray'. To ask God's help. That's all very fine, but when the floodgates run over, when the river has burst its banks, when the storms of life are tossing and turning you about, when you see tiny babies die in the night and whole families killed in road accidents, well, it becomes too much. Nothing makes sense. And then you look at the heavens and the Milky Way, and see how it spreads forever and ever with millions of specks of stars and planets and we know not what, you just wonder about it all."

We stood gazing for a while. I thought of Woodleigh Hall and the whispers in corners, the petty meannesses; and my belongings scrutinised and tossed about, the huge garden I was beginning to love. And Gerald. Especially Gerald.

"All I know, Simon, is that the important thing this instant is how cold I'm feeling."

He burst into Caring Man.

"How thoughtless of me. Here, Philly, have another swig."

"I really think I ought to be getting back. Gerald just might be worried about me."

"Not all joy and bliss in the happy halls of Woodleigh?"

"What do you think? A brother who's a cross between Caliban and the Hunchback of Notre Dame and a sister who's first cousin to the Wicked Witch of the West, not to mention a husband who's really married to his word processor."

"Well, you know where we are if you want to chat."

So much for feeling I'd an ear right then. Canon Goodhew didn't want to know. No wonder Gladys was slightly turned off reality; she probably had to paddle her own canoe.

He turned and went down the little hill. Everyone wants someone to listen but no one reciprocates. One's woes are left to oneself.

Gerald was still cross the next day and didn't come down for breakfast. Mort and Pimmsy had eaten all the bacon and black pudding when my back was turned and left a hard, greasy egg. Considerate as always. No more breakfasts in future I decided. I would have muesli in my room before I got up and they could fend for themselves.

At least the garden was under control. All the brambles had been pulled or received a severe setback. Old Stoat, the septuagenarian gardener

Gerald persuaded to give me a hand, brought barrow-loads of dung from the cattle sheds.

"Unusual name – Stoat," I said in my pleasant voice, in desperate need of some human contact.

He gave me an extremely unpleasant look, one I felt capable of but usually restrained myself.

"Better'n 'Weasel'!" He pointed the rake in my direction like a lethal weapon. "Know the difference 'atween a weasel 'n' a stoat?" he asked.

I confessed ignorance, though I felt certain it had to do with the shape of their snout.

"Well," he said, raising the rake a smidgen higher, "a weasel's weaselly recognised 'n' a stoat's stotally different!"

He laughed like a drain. I stuck the fork into the heap of dung.

Within a month we had transplanted four thousand Elsanta strawberries, designer-bred to cope with every conceivable mishap from dirty fruit to heat stress. However, they failed to breed out the flavour by some lucky fluke, though they couldn't compare with Royal Sovereign. Dung being best for strawberries, we ladled it on. Every time Mr Stoat came puffing along with the wheelbarrow, I thought he was going to have a heart attack.

"At your age you should be taking things easy, have your feet up," I said to him, trying not to sound critical.

"May as well be dead if that's the case. The

missus'd hate me round her feet — only two rooms in our cottage."

"How on earth did you rear so many children?" His family of ten was legendary.

"We all snuggled up together. No need for hot water bottles. None of them ever had a nightmare in their lives. Always someone to hand to quiet them down. Mind you, it were girls at top of bed and boys at bottom. All gone now. No little pink heads poking from under covers anymore."

"You obviously miss them."

"Not a bit. Nothing but what I expected. All little bonhams grow up and go to market."

Stoat's fatalism was a bit trying, so I took a break and left him to his bacon sandwich and flask of beer.

There wasn't a grain of coffee in the kitchen when I got there, not even a tea bag. Unless I replenished the stocks, it seemed nothing was bought, though Pimmsy never seemed to go short of his tipple. I decided to tell Gerald it was all a bit much and climbed the attic stairs to his hideaway. I heard the click of keys as I came to the door and the sound of the phone ringing. I waited outside.

"Maria!" he exclaimed. "How is the world treating you? You got it. Good. I'm glad you like it. Lunch? Well, how about some day next week — at the usual place?"

Indeed! I went in.

"Why Pips! Anything wrong?"

"Why does there have to be something wrong if I visit you in your hideyhole? I thought we were married, shared our lives together."

"For a start, there are some things one cannot share – or even some things one shouldn't share."

"Really? Here's me thinking it was a partnership."

"Don't be silly, Philippa. Of course, we're together in all this."

So who was Maria? My pride refused to allow me to enquire.

"Pardon my intrusion on the flow of creative juices but I'm thoroughly fed up with these good-for-nothing, selfish, uncivilised relations of yours that never bid one the time of day and eat and drink rings round them to their heart's content. I'm eating out tonight. You may want to do the same. If so, I'll see you in the hall at half past seven." I took off before he had a chance to demur.

Old Stoat looked at me oddly on my return to the garden.

"How do you like Woodleigh Hall, then?" he asked quietly.

"To be honest, Mr Stoat, not much." I didn't dare say another word. For all I knew, Mr Stoat might be a respecter of confidences but there was no need to let the world know what a miserable, newly married wife to a famous mystery-story writer I was.

By quarter to eight there was still no sign of Gerald, so I went off by myself. Dining alone is fine when you've no partner in the background, and doubly painful when you do but he chooses to spend it with his word processor – or Maria. I hardly tasted the beautiful sliced pigeon salad or the perfectly cooked guinea fowl in port which followed. The waiter did his best to cheer me up, offering little *petit fours* "with the Chef's compliments" and as much coffee as I wished. Even the wine didn't have a serious dent in it. At that stage, I knew I was in a bad way. What on earth could I do? Just leave them all to it and go home? Take the chip from Gerald's computer? Put a kitchen into my bedroom and cook to my heart's content? I hate to fail at anything. There was always the parish council, of course. I could throw myself into it, body and soul, and hope Gerald would miss me so much he would come begging forgiveness, lavish flowers upon me, kick old Pimmsy and Caliban into the lodge, ban the Wicked Witch from the estate and run the farm properly. That sounded like a better plan. I finished the rest of the Chablis in next to no time and demolished the *petit fours* with gusto. The waiter gave me a wink as he handed me the bill.

Gerald was fast asleep on top of my embroidered heirloom. I squeezed under the covers as unobtrusively as possible. He jumped bolt upright.

"Philippa! I thought we were to go out to dinner?"

"That was several hours ago," I said curling to one side and nestling into the pillow.

"Thought I'd just lie down for an instant to rest my eyes. I'd no idea . . ."

If he thought I was going to forgive, he had another think coming.

"Have you been out? Alone?"

I grunted.

"That can't have been much fun? Maybe it was?"

I was busy counting sheep.

"I'm very sorry, Pips," he leant over me just as a sheep was in mid-air over a gate. "I was really looking forward to an evening together. You've every right to be cross."

"I don't need your permission to be cross. I'd a very pleasant evening, thank you."

"Did you really? Without me?"

There was a tiny note of hurt in his voice that pleased me no end. Maddeningly, moisture gathered in my eyes. Before I had time to wipe it away, he turned, got out of bed and came to kneel by my side.

"So, you still like me, a teeny-weeny bit?" he asked.

"That's the worst part, Gerald. I like you a lot, and I hate the loss of independence."

"You couldn't have put it better, Pips. It's difficult for me too."

He ran his hands through my hair and across the back of my neck in a way that made me half glad to be alive.

"I suppose it's OK so long as we're both suffering," he smiled and I smiled and the room began to spin and I chased the sheep back into the field and told them I'd call for them some other time.

An hour or two later, when the cymbals stopped clashing, Gerald became aware of other appetites.

"I'm absolutely ravenous. You keep the bed warm and I'll get myself a sandwich."

I knew it was all lies. I'm simply not enough for him.

He came back carrying a tray laden with jars of pickle, a lump of salami and some ripe Camembert. I buttered some slices of French bread while he opened the pickles.

"A bit quiet our Pips? *Post-coitus animus tristus* – or something even worse?"

"Who is Maria?" Out it slipped, the thing that had been burning inside.

He looked startled, which frightened me even more.

"Oh, Maria Kershaw – my agent, the one person in my life I have to be nice to, regardless."

"And you *have* to take her to lunch of course."

"Indeed. Costs me a fortune. An appetite like a hippopotamus and a face to match."

"Gerald! I've never heard you sound so insulting. Can't you change agents?"

"Well, to be brief – or my pickle will get cold – my previous agent came with us on the trip to the Himalayas. Took a fancy to a Sherpa. What with too much *chang* and a sudden storm she got slightly chilled and died."

"You sound almost angry."

"Very. She was a lovely person. Got me my first book published. So, out of a sort of loyalty to her, I stayed with her partner, Maria. Though my loyalty wears a bit thin at times."

An enormous pile of salami, cheese and pickled vegetables disappeared through his soft lips. Lucky food.

"What are you staring at, Philippa?"

Of course, I forgot his defensiveness about food.

"Not a thing. Just wondering why your family can't be even half as nice as you."

"Look, Philippa," he speared a stray onion, "why can't you just ignore them as I do? Just avoid them as much as possible and observe the barest courtesies."

Even that sounded like hard work.

༄ Chapter Five ༃

"Can everybody see?" Gladys barked at the assembled crew. She held the worm bin out for inspection.

"Ugh!" A general cry went up into the frosty air.

"They don't bite," I soothed. Not yet anyway. Perhaps they could be trained ..

The Canon came forward, wearing his serious, clerical look. He raised his arms and lowered them again, muttering something in Latin over the bin.

"*Woodleigh Vermiculture*, a division of Woodleigh Enterprises, is now officially launched," he said, handing the bin to Mr Manifold, who was now custodian of the "worm cast" from which all later editions of *Eisenia foetida* were to be hatched. He gave instructions on how to prepare our bins.

"Any container will do but a dustbin's as handy as anything."

"But they cost a few quid!" A small, thin man shouted from the back of the group.

"Six pound isn't much capital to make of an investment. Cut out pub for a night and you've got it."

Mr Manifold was no respecter of habits. To some people, not having a pint for a night was like asking a cripple to climb Mount Everest.

"There is an easy purchase scheme, all the same," Gladys Goodhew hastily added. "A pound a week for six weeks."

This seemed to animate the onlookers.

"In bottom of bin ye put a layer of shredded newspaper and dampen it a bit. Then you put in your worms," he lifted a wriggling handful. Gladys put her hankie to her mouth. I could foresee the Canon having to do that particular part.

"We all need grub," Mr Manifold continued.

"Some more'n others," a cheeky teenager with a frill for a skirt twittered.

"An' there's some what could do with a bit of filling out," Mr Manifold said to the delight of a few. Not a man to be trifled with.

"Next goes the grub. All your peelings, chicken wings, plate scrapings – toss 'em in."

"Do worms have teeth, Mr M? Do they eat bones?" the thin man at the back enquired.

"Don't be daft. They don't *eat* bones – just suck 'em dry. Ready for grinding into bonemeal."

I groaned at the thought of this production offshoot and hoped no one noticed.

"Feed 'em every day, a layer of newspaper and a layer of food. In six months you'll have a bucket of compost."

"Six ruddy months!" the thin man said.

"Nature takes time to work," Mr Manifold said quietly. "It takes one thousand years to make an inch of topsoil."

Gladys nodded as if to say "There you are!" The thin man was not impressed.

"Rather watch paint dry," and shuffled off to the bookmakers.

I suddenly had a brainwave.

"The first person to bring a bucket-full of worm compost will get a Christmas turkey courtesy of Woodleigh Hall," I found myself saying.

That cheered them up.

"Go over it again, Mr Manifold, please," a fat, ruddy-faced woman said.

An hour later, everyone had dispersed, two dozen Red Wigglers a-piece clutched tightly in a plastic bag. Mr Manifold looked pleased, moved almost.

"Great sight that," he said, putting a sleeve to his cheek. "Nice to know you can do summat for folk."

Beneath every large man there's a tiny, helpful one trying to get out.

Loneliness is a creeping paralysis. It begins with

empty hands and arms and ends with a cold heart. Evening time, as the casserole simmered away, the table set and Gerald still glued to the VDU, was worst. I walked to the edge of the ha-ha, the dry ditch that prevented any four-footed creature from putting a toe on the garden, and watched the sun disappear, a flaming ball in a pink sky. Knowing that it was the same sun going down on my little farm in Ireland was torture, as if a huge room inside me was sealed, not allowed to see the light of day. Perhaps it would be wise to go back home after all, run from the petty meanness of Mort and Pimmsy and the bossiness of Big Sis. As soon as the thought saw the light of day, I knew it was no answer. One may as well hide in a windowless room and never answer the door. And that was not living. We were given life to live it, to make of it what we could.

"More lamb?" I asked Gerald, away as usual, solving his mystery puzzles in the circus of his mind.

He winced as he came to, as if reality were painful.

"No. No, thank you, Philippa."

We were back to formalities. Trouble with having a nick-name. You knew exactly when people were annoyed with you.

"Did you enjoy it?" I enquired.

"The lamb? Yes, yes, of course. You cooked it."

"That is not what I asked."

"Well, to be perfectly honest, it could have done

with a bit of bay leaf, perhaps another clove of garlic. I always feel lamb responds well to a few handfuls of barley."

"Really."

I let the silence fill the room and didn't try to justify my wanton cooking. Perhaps I should rejuvenate the macrobiotic dishes I learnt in Dublin, serve up some helpings of miso soup with slimy seaweed, unsweetened sour apple topped with nut cream. Help him to appreciate anything.

Such is love. It perishes on the rock of reality.

"Well, I'd better get going and let you get back to your word processor."

He seemed startled.

"Can we not have a chat, sit by the fire and just be together?"

"I thought that's what we'd been trying to do during the past hour over this dismal meal that didn't meet with your expectations."

"Now, Pippy. Don't be so aggressive. Can't a fellow say what he likes and dislikes?"

Absolutely not. Forbidden in the first year of marriage.

"Of course," I replied, wishing I still smoked, whereupon I could pull on a cigarette and blow the smoke out with vengeance. Talking about likes and dislikes is fine, all going well. But when everything was topsy-turvy, when a girl felt *de trop*, as if no one cared, then people should be more indulgent.

"Really, Gerald, I must go. Important parish council work. Must help those less fortunate."

I could feel very hurt eyes bore into me. But I was determined not to give in. I was infinitely more hurt than him.

The worms were proving very popular. Some people could swear they knew each one by name and had bets taken on who could demolish the most peelings in the shortest possible time.

"Can't see this worm business taking off in the cities," Simey said, as he peered into his pilgrim bottle to see how the supplies stood.

I raised an enquiring eyebrow.

"All these ready-prepared vegetables," he said taking a quick swig. "Poor, tired housewife comes home from a day slogging in the office and hasn't the energy to peel a potato or scrape a carrot."

"That's an idea! Why don't we prepare the vegetables and feed the worms with the peelings? We could have mountains of peelings, a giant wormery."

"Here, have a sip of this before you get carried away."

"Thirsty so early in the evening?" Gladys suddenly descended upon us.

I offered her the flask. She recoiled as if from sin.

Simey stood to attention, sucked his lips in and out.

"The worms need feeding, Simon!" Gladys said.

Like a lamb to the slaughter, Simey lifted his feet and marched to the rectory worm bin.

Gladys was certainly worth watching. Oh to have such power . . .

"Nice to have you on your own, for a change, Philippa. You seem to be so busy with farming and cooking and now this worm business. Come on over to the rectory. I've the kettle simmering – we've just about time for a nice cup of tea and a chat."

The rectory was spartan and clean. Wood panelling crept half-way up the walls and then gave way to lime green paint. Eighteenth century prints depicting *Feeding the Poor* and *A Dying child gets Comfort from Prayer* hung on either side of a mahogany door. Gladys ushered me through this into a room that was filled with the watery light of early winter. There was even a sunbeam holding dust mites dancing away for all they were worth.

"Have a seat while I get the tea things. All you'll find to read are copies of Bishop Berkeley's sermons which Simon has used to good effect for over twenty years. Never a one to agonise over Sunday morning. He made a collection of sermons when he was a student, one for each Sunday in the year, two for funerals – one for children and the other adults – oh! and one for weddings. Only one. About love."

She stopped in the middle of piling a stack of sticks that looked as though they'd been taken from a jackdaw's nest, all roughly the same thickness and length.

"Love?" I enquired, though I felt it was a mistake.

"About how it's not what the songs and the films and the books would have us believe. It's not enough to say 'I love you' and then expect something magical to happen. It's not fair to the other person to say: I'm relying on you to make me happy."

"One can surely make some sort of effort. Sounds as if no one is obliged to do anything, Gladys."

"Oh, absolutely. But one mustn't expect the effort to be returned."

She bent her head over the cup. "Like Simon and I. You'll have gathered we're not . . . we don't, you know, enjoy . . . nothing like the gay abandon of the early days!"

I sipped the weak tea. Gladys economises by using only one tea bag and dunking it into each cup. She probably dries them in the airing cupboard and then donates them to the poor.

"It must be wonderful for you, Philippa, in the first flush of love – and all that."

Delirious, but no sense in boasting.

"Well, Gladys, we'd better get a move on. I can't

stay long at the meeting. A few sheep are arriving in the early hours of the morning, so I need an early bed."

"Do you never take it easy, Philippa?"

"Not if I can help it. The less time I spend thinking, the better."

The following day, the two hundred sheep I had bought were decanted in less than an hour. I saw the shadows of Mort and Pimmsy lurking about the yard but neither came to give a hand. Old Stoat was there with his stick and between us we managed to encourage the sheep to travel northwards, towards the grass ley. As soon as they felt the lush pasture under their feet, they set to, nibbling away.

"Good condition for Welsh mountainy sheep," he said leaning, across the gate. "Let's hope their homing instinct got buggered on the way."

"Why do you say that, Mr Stoat?"

"'Cos I ain't in no fit condition to travel after them to Wales."

Poor Stoat doesn't realise how lazy the modern breeds are.

We walked towards the garden just as the sun was disappearing in angry redness.

"At least we'll have some nice spring lamb with mint sauce courtesy of the garden and perhaps a few strawberries and cream." I felt almost optimistic. Dream on, oh fool.

As we reached the garden, a riderless horse streaked through the gate and galloped on down the driveway.

"Wasn't that Mortimer's horse? What on earth was it doing in the garden?" I asked Stoat.

"Making a right bloody mess."

The newly planted strawberry runners were either buried deeply under a hoof print or sitting on top of the ridge, torn from the ground.

"All our work, Mr Stoat!"

"Aye. Can't say as I'm surprised."

"You mean it was done deliberately?"

"Folks round 'ere are known for their little meannesses. Twisted minds take delight in seeing other folks suffer."

"I knew there was jealousy. But this . . . this is extreme. We'll have to do something!"

Mr Stoat shrugged his shoulders, gathered up the tools and walked towards the shed.

I aimed a swift kick at the mint bucket and stubbed my toe. I was just in the mood to tackle Gerald.

"What do you expect me to do about it, Philippa?" Gerald asked when I told him of the destruction. "You know as well as I do that Mort is not a fully paid up member of the human race."

"But he can't be allowed to get away with this, Gerald."

"Saying anything to him will merely get a snigger and denial."

"So why on earth am I bothering to do anything if it's sabotaged?"

"It's one of the hazards of being around here. He obviously resents his slapdash ways being interrupted."

To my amazement, Gerald actually got up and turned off the word processor.

"It looks as if I will have to show myself a bit more, protect you so he realises he has two people to contend with. I'll give you a hand to put back the strawberries and we'll make the gate so narrow that nothing except your elegant body can get through it."

I loved him all over again. So much for Gladys saying we can never expect anything from anyone.

Over the phone, Gerald ordered some bricks and a small quantity of readymix. While waiting their arrival, we set to with dibbers, re-planting the strawberries. He looked like a reincarnation of Grizzly Adams, his muscled shoulders glowing on either side of his dungarees.

"Gerald," I said, running my fingers along his collar bone and down through the divisions in his hairy chest, "you're such a mixture of lofty intellect and primitive man. Digging soil is like parting seaweed to you. I'm intrigued."

"Well, I'll let you into a little secret. I slip out of our bed in the dead of night, meet up with Stoat on the landing and the pair of us go for a ten mile jog till daybreak."

No wonder he's not able for me in the mornings.

By the time we'd had our tea break, the bricks and cement had arrived. We measured the opening into the garden with Gerald's frame, as he was just slightly taller than me but using Stoat's girth, as he was undoubtedly the more muscled. We finished before the cement had dried to a solid lump.

"Now!" said Gerald, scraping the stray bits of cement from the bricks, "I defy any animal to get through that!"

I looked at our handiwork.

"Just one little thing – poor old wheelbarrow won't be able to either."

With the remainder of the cement on his trowel Gerald decorated his masterpiece with the most bizarre design.

Life was bliss for at least a day or two after that. Mortido was away galloping his poor horse most of the time; even Sybil had flown to climes more receptive of her charms. Pimmsy mellowed enough to chat occasionally. On his own he was almost human.

"So many changes around here since I was a lad helping my father till the land." He leaned against the open doorway and lit a cigarette. "Smaller fields then. Lots of hedges and trees. 'Grub 'em all out,' the Ministry said. Now we're being paid to put them all back. They're paying people to grow weeds instead of grain. What happens if the crop fails?"

"Nothing like an empty stomach to galvanise people. That's what started the French Revolution after all."

"Except that all our grain is used to feed cattle. Enough to drive you to drink."

I didn't think he needed an excuse.

He slipped inside, leaving me on the steps. The view was soothing. Rolling parkland stretched to the horizon, golden in the evening light. The sheep were visible, white balls moving steadily, mowing the grass as they went.

"First of day," Pimmsy returned, handed me a sherry and tossed back half a glass of gin.

"Not good for the liver," I said as gently as I could.

"What the heck would I preserve it for?"

"Difficult to manage without one."

"I'm on the way out anyway. May as well enjoy myself."

"Are you really enjoying yourself?"

He gave me a filthy look and swallowed the rest in one gulp.

"It was losing Dorothy, Gerald's mother, that ruined everything." He sat beside me on the step and played with his hands, putting the fingers of one against the back of the other. I was finding it difficult to summon any sympathy for him. He had done a poor PR job on himself since my arrival at Woodleigh.

"Dorothy was a character. Gerald takes after her. I'm afraid the others take after me."

Such confession was heartening. I was beginning to find some warmth.

"It must have been sad to lose her."

"March it was, a cold day to begin with. I stoked the Aga – it was going in those days – and made coffee. She liked her coffee, two mugs of it before she got up. I put the cat's food out and, queer thing, it wouldn't touch it. Just stared at me. They say cats sense things. Anyway, I didn't pay much heed and went upstairs with the coffee. I pulled back the curtains.

"'Dry morning anyway,' I said to Dot. 'Maybe we'll get pruning the blackcurrants before you set to work.' There was no reply. That wasn't unusual; she'd often be thinking about her sculpture or something and wouldn't hear. But when I went towards her with the coffee, there was something funny about the way her arm was hanging out of the bed and the stillness of her face, though her eyes were open. I tried and tried to make her come to life, pulled the clothes up round her, rubbed her cold hands, even shouted at her. But then, it was no use, no use at all."

We were silent for an age after that. The evening was black, the moon in its last quarter just rising behind the house.

"So, Philippa. I must apologise for my family. Not the most prepossessing of mortals, but they're all I've got."

"Still no need for them to be quite so obnoxious," I said, vainly hoping to influence slightly but we often prefer to ignore the evil before us than face the black void of loneliness.

Pimmsy got up and, without another word, shuffled into the house.

◖ Chapter Six ◗

A return letter from Emily:

Dear Philly

Paid a suspicious visit to the farm – Andy and Gorry or Glorry or whatever mockery of a name she has, took ages to come to the door – she said they'd been doing aerobics, but you can tell. Not a bad looking girl but when her face is all red she looks quite coarse. Even with the chill in the air she had on a queer sort of butter muslin blouse thing that left nothing to the imagination. The yard was filthy, a sick pig in one of the outhouses and a barrelful of apples going soft in the porch. You wouldn't know the kitchen! I don't want to worry you, P., but it was very untidy. Peelings, dirty plates, clothes everywhere – wet things draped over the backs of chairs, black-looking things soaking, lacy bits and pieces hanging over the range – there wasn't a space free. In the corner beside your beautiful pine dresser a few dozen ducks were paddling about in filthy sawdust, climbing on top of each other with the cold. I told Andy you'd get a shock if you saw the state of the place – he said he'd clean it up whenever you were on your way.

Dickie in good form – onions beginning to sprout, TG. I've decided to do a women's studies course in Ballinamore. Dickie's against it – thinks I'll become one of those feminists. I told him the teacher was a straightforward married woman like myself with a husband and children and it didn't seem to do her any harm. Maybe it'll stop me wanting to murder those onions. The Greene's are on top of the world – little Tommy is mad about them – but then I suppose a baby doesn't care who its daddy is so long as it feels sure of its next meal. Got the fright of my life though when I called – a cousin of theirs in America sent on the latest things for fathers to help them get bonded with the child. A kind of plastic bosom that hangs around the neck and dangles milk-filled things on either side. A bit like the real thing, but Percy says you've to be careful not to let ultra violet near it or the whole thing cracks. Thank God mother nature has something left up her sleeve.

Haven't seen Seamus or Noreen recently. They went to Aran for a week but I never heard how they got on. Clara is planning to go to Morocco again for Christmas. Miss you at the Archaeological *meetings – not the same atmosphere at all. Sophia continues to come and gives us all a tin ear. No wonder her husband is going deaf – though they say he's got piped music in his hearing aid.*

Better go – a soufflé in the oven. Dickie's taken to this posh sort of food since the holiday in the south of France – and invites Percy to partake at every turn. I suppose it's nice to have a good friend, especially for a man.

All the best. Miss you,
Em

"Poor old Emily. Yes, I'll bet those two are seeing more of each other in every sense of the word. Better than being lonely, I suppose."

"Do you really think so?" Gerald asked.

One of the most inconvenient things about marriage is a girl can't express an opinion or talk to herself without interruptions. Four-footed friends never answer back, just love you to death.

"Actually, Gerald, I was talking to myself."

"Huh! I see. Who better to talk to? Certainly not your husband."

"Men always seem ready to take umbrage. You'll have to grow a more impervious skin."

"I'm not 'men'," Philippa. I'm me. I refuse to be lumped with the rest of humanity."

"We have a very crude old saw in my part of the world for that sort of egocentrism."

"Bad news in the letter, Philippa?"

I suppose I was waspish, missing home probably. But no sense in admitting to it.

He got up from his marmalade and cheese sandwich and went off in high dudgeon. Just when I'd needed a shoulder to lean on, to weep for my little farm and get cross about it being badly treated, I sabotaged any comfort. We're at our worst when we need each other most.

Stoat was waiting for me, as usual, with a rosy, beatific smile across his face. It seemed to say "No matter what happens, I think it's all a lark".

"Let's scout out those few hedgerows that survived the flail, Stoat, and see whether there's any berries or fruit. It looks like crab apple country to me."

Billows of smoke rose from his pipe. He nodded.

In the field bordered by the wood the hedges had been allowed to grow with abandon. Rowan, thorn, hazel were there, their fruits taken by birds and squirrels.

"Oh look, Stoat, a spindle tree." It was a mass of beautiful fruits.

"What we used to cut when we butchered a pig. It made the best skewers, hard and straight."

"That's of course why it was used in spindles. The fruit is poisonous except to birds."

"I sure as 'ell won't be eating it! Now that crab apple is a different thing."

He strode off in that deliberate, cart-horse way of his and presently stopped at a bedraggled looking tree.

"Been in the wars," I said, patting its twisted branches, some torn by wind.

I followed Stoat's gaze up into the tree's crown. At the top, untouchable, was a cascade of apples, golden in the shafts of sunlight.

"A schoolboy's temptation that," he said.

He picked a heavy piece of branch from the ground and, standing back, slung it up into the tree. A trickle of fruit tumbled onto the ground. He threw his stick again and we shortly had enough apples for several pounds of jelly.

"Now you can see why my hat's so big," he said. Its sides seemed to grow the more it was filled.

"Of course the American Indians used to bury them until spring to sweeten them up," I informed him, "though in this part of the world it looks as if they were cooked *with* other food as they've found pips embedded in prehistoric pottery. I've a friend Eddie, an archaeologist, who's an absolute walking encyclopaedia on the subject."

I wondered how Eddie was getting along with his very own primitive, my sister Aggie, and whether he'd managed to save her from herself and wean her off the gin. It was the skin and bone that appealed to the archaeologist in him.

"Can't say I know much about book learning but

I do know about folk. If I'm not mistaken that's Master Mortimer behind that oak tree with its branch dipping into the ditch."

Sure enough, a now familiar shape loomed there, making little attempt to hide itself. That was the thing about Mortido, he wanted you to *know* he was watching.

"I think we'll make tracks, Mrs Gerald, all the same."

Just what I'd been thinking.

I washed and de-stalked the crab apples and put them in a dish in the oven. By morning all the juices would have poured out, leaving the skin and pulp. With ale, sugar and a pinch of spice added to the pulp I could make Lambs Wool, the drink Puck made in *Midsummer Night's Dream*, so that he could "bob against his mistress's lips". I doubted if Gerald would be interested. He's really a wine person.

"What a gorgeous colour, Philippa, tiny golden apples like thine orbs," Gerald burst in upon me, bent one knee and grabbed my hand to kiss. I was obviously forgiven for not being perfect.

"Dearest sweet, if mine orbs were *that* colour I think thou hast better get me to a physician," I replied.

"Let love be thy physic and embrace me tight."

"I knew it was all some sort of ploy to get me where you want me." I still marvelled at the softness of his lips, the acid, male odour of his neck and body.

"You know, Gerald," I said pulling back a little, "you don't have to do this just to get fed."

"I wish you'd said that weeks ago. Here's me exhausting myself just to get a square meal."

"It's bread and jam tonight," I fibbed.

"Well, that's a shame," Gerald said chewing on the crust. "I thought we would dine out, seeing it's a special day. But now my appetite will be ruined."

Not mine, however.

"What a very good idea."

Half an hour later we were Chez Pierre, where the tablecloths are of Irish linen with drawn threadwork and a centre of embroidered vegetables. The food was almost as good.

"While there is nothing to beat home cooking, that is, *your* cooking, Philippa, it's nice to see what the rest of the world spends its money on. Don't stint yourself."

The pike looked tempting, a most under-rated fish, except by the French, who smother it in butter and poach it for hours.

"So, this is a special treat tonight?"

"Yes, Pippy. I'm so excited. And it's all your fault. I've just written the best story yet, thanks to your inspiration."

I dreaded to ask whether it had anything to do with . . . anything private.

"Aren't you going to ask me? It does worry me that you don't seem at all interested in reading any of my work."

Not another row. Pike takes a lot of energy to digest. I should have ordered milk pudding.

"Of course I am, darling. I'm just trying not to be too nosy."

"In that case . . . but don't let me run on and on. Writers tend to be egomaniacs, as obsessed with their creations as an alcoholic with the taste of drink."

"Indulge yourself, my dear. After all, you're paying."

"That makes it sound very commercial. Do I really have to buy your time?"

Perhaps a glass of milk would have been more appropriate.

"Gerald. Just stop. Yes, I'm happy to listen to your story. No, you don't have to 'buy' my time – that was a feeble joke."

"Very."

A platter of *crudités* arrived to dispel the gloom. The centre was a splash of bright red – a collection of cherries stuffed with Camembert, or was it Brie?

I reached for one.

"Philippa! Can't you wait?"

It was my turn to sulk. A naughty child caught with her fingers in the bonbon dish. Gerald obviously never heard of spontaneity. Dampen that and a girl may as well give up the ghost.

"It's all yours," I said. I sat back and looked at the other diners. A retired stockbroker – you can tell from the hump in the back – and his wife were working their way through a mountain of pasta. At their age easier to chew than steak au poivre. In a corner sat a young couple, she all tinsel and lip gloss and he with meticulously coiffed hair, stiff with gel. He had soft, kind eyes like John Major.

I turned back to the *crudités*. Gerald had carefully halved everything, down to the last shred of orange zest. What the heck! A girl could starve if she sulked long enough.

Gerald gave me his wide grin and shining eyes.

"So, what wonderful idea did I give you for your story?" I asked, casting pride to the wind.

"Worms. In the story I had a body that I had to get rid of but that had to be discovered later. So, what better way than have it thrown into a worm bin! The bones are discovered by my eco-aware detective, who decided they're a bit too big for chicken and the wrong shape for a horse. Of course the skull is a dead giveaway, if you'll pardon the expression."

"Are these comedies, Gerald?"

"How come you manage to say the one thing that hits a fellow in the solar plexus?"

"I didn't know you even had one! I simply asked a question."

One waiter removed the empty dishes while

another deposited a *brochet au beurre blanc* for me and a *blanquette de veau cordon bleu* for his nibs.

We looked at each other through the steam. What beautiful hands Gerald has, square and manly yet delicate and expressive.

"Sorry, Pips. As well as being egomaniacs, writers tend to be as vulnerable as a woman in the arms of Casanova. No, my books aren't intended to be comical. Though I wouldn't rule that out .."

He drifted off into that writer's dreamland where the little cogs and wheels whirr and click and spin their magic. It was where my loved one was happy, if not happiest and I was left alone, to think and plan and feel miserable. Were we compatible merely in our incompatibility? I tucked into my dinner and left the imponderables for a safer time. No sense in wasting a half decent piece of fish or a fine dish of truffles.

"Pips. We can't go on sniping at each other," Gerald said, dabbing his coffee-moistened lips.

"Sniping? Is that what you're doing to me?"

He looked at me, that hurt expression magnified a thousand-fold, his mouth slightly open. If only I could tell him how much I loved him, how I didn't care about the rest, who won or lost in our little *contretemps*. But there was the "war of the sexes", where one slip and you would be condemned to everlasting punishment.

"As I intimated, Philippa," he said, straightening.

We were now back to formalities.

"I think we're sniping at each other."

"It was you who mentioned 'sniping'," I reminded gently.

I'd got him there.

"Only a manner of expression."

And there we were, at a dead end.

"Gerald, couldn't we just . . . forget whatever it was and start again?"

"No. I'd like to finish this."

Exactly what, I wasn't sure. Short of getting up and leaving the last half of my brandy truffle, there wasn't a thing I could do. Gerald continued a dissertation on how we should be civil towards each other and respectful and even 'cheerful' whenever possible. I was busy watching the way his brow curved when he was particularly serious, how his lips came together when he made a statement that hung in the air like a poem, the way he put his tongue between his lips and momentarily moistened them. It was his arms I ached for, not his head on my plate.

"What sort of woman was your mother?" I asked.

He looked at me, trying to decide whether I was being flippant or in earnest.

"A creative person, with little energy for chatting or arguing. She put it all into her work."

"Ah," I said.

"What is that 'ah' supposed to mean?"

"Just that – an 'ah' expressing how interesting. 'Show me the man and I'll show you his mother' Nellie used to say when we were children. That was why she never married – either the prospective husband's mother was dead or she was very much alive and kicking. She ached for an orphan into whose life she could enter as the long-lost mother, without competition from the living or dead. But it never happened. Nellie's loss was our gain. She gave us all the love she had for ten husbands, more love than our own mother was capable or willing to bestow."

"Good old Nellie, but pity about your mother. Have another truffle to cheer you up, Pips."

"Why not?" Food was a welcome substitute for loss.

Another dish of delicious mouthfuls arrived.

"You seem slightly subdued? Truffles all right?"

"Perfect. I was thinking about my childhood. Not a good idea after a nice meal in good company."

"That's OK. It's when we're relaxed that past torments jump up to grab us by the throat. I find it happens when I've just finished a satisfying chapter and I take five minutes to drink a cup of coffee and stare out the window. Then it all comes rushing back."

"All?"

"Well, all the bad bits. Mother busy with her

sculpture, father out tractoring or drinking in the barn. Mortimer and Sybil torturing some hapless animal in the yard or making mud pies to throw at me. They say a miserable childhood is the best start a writer could have. If it doesn't poleaxe you in the meantime, that is."

"Do you think that's true?"

"Well, here I am. A writer. And you, it seems, are a poet."

"That's a bit grandiose for my feeble verses. They merely articulate the scratch of the bow on the string, they go no deeper."

"Give it time. Once the volcano finds a fissure, however tiny, it rumbles and pushes to get through it."

For the umpteenth time I wondered what I did to deserve such a saint.

All was dark and quiet at Woodleigh on our return – except for the ringing of the phone.

"It's for you," Gerald shouted as I closed the back door on a very cross cat.

"Hi, Philly. Sorry to bother you so late."

Eddie. I said nothing to relieve his embarrassment.

"It's Ag. Really gone for it this time. Had a few friends round and they all brought a bottle of something. She was going fine till she hit the ouzo some idiot brought back from a holiday. People should know better."

"Well, Eddie, they don't know our Ag's capacity. These things are meant to languish on shelves and perhaps come in contact with a trifle now and again."

"I know, I know. Anyway. She's bad."

"Hospital is what she needs."

"She'll go mad! She said if I ever put her in hospital she'd never speak to me again."

That might be the best thing.

"Take your choice, Eddie: hospital or death."

"Yeh, well, I'll be in touch."

Gerald handed me a note. "Worm trouble. Pse call chez Gamble soonest." Simon.

"Sure you haven't bitten off more than you can, em, chew with this worm business?"

"There is nothing scientific about raising worms. Just shovel the grub at them and away they go." If only Agatha were as easy to fix.

Of course, that wasn't quite what the vermiculturalists in Woodleigh were doing.

I sped off to Mrs Gamble, leaving an unhappy Gerald on the doorstep. A girl has to feel she can help *someone*.

"You've forgotten the shredded paper, Mrs Gamble," I said, having surveyed the rotting worm corpses. "They need it to mop up the wet, otherwise the whole thing gets sloppy and stinky. Like living in wet clothes – how would you like it?"

I looked at her in earnest. Anyone who mistreats a worm isn't fit to live.

"There's an 'ell of a difference between me 'n a worm," she said, arms folded, her eyes narrowing like a snake. "They're only dirt, after all".

"Dirt?" I enquired, though I should really have left well alone. "Do you realise it's 'dirt' like worms that our planet relies on for its survival? If it weren't for the worms in the soil we'd have nothing to eat? It's a miracle, despite modern farming practices, that a single worm survives to reproduce, make its worm casts and enrich the soil in the process. Give those worms of yours a dry place to live and they won't know themselves."

"Could do with a bit of dryness meself," she began to cry.

"No need to get upset. Get me a newspaper and I'll help you."

She went inside the little cottage and I followed. Though slightly bigger than Stoat's, it wasn't nearly as comfortable. The air smelt of damp, like a disused gym full of stale plimsolls. A child was crying in an adjoining room.

"Truth is, Mrs Gerald, we don't have no newspapers here. Me an' Flora, we just stayed on when 'er dad left for Kuwait. Bought his ticket with all our savings and the silver teaspoons me mother gave me before she died."

This stopped me in my tracks. Stolen spoons, no

newspapers, an absent father juggled together to form one thing in my head: poverty and starvation.

"Is Flora hungry?"

"Starving. Only had porridge tonight and she hates it. She wouldn't touch it."

I loved the child already. Porridge is an abomination.

"You can stay at Woodleigh Hall until we see what can be done. There's enough room there to fit the whole village. Flora needs food and heat. You grab what you need and I'll see to the worms."

Supper seemed to be well and truly over by the time we got to Woodleigh. The kitchen smelt of people and fried sausages. Not a scrap left for anyone. I grabbed a quiche from the freezer and put it in the oven. I opened the biscuit tin and offered Flora a caramel square. She just looked at them.

"Go on," I encouraged. "They get all blue mouldy if they're not eaten and have to be given to the worms."

She took two. Not behind the door when it comes to looking after herself. I gave her another one just to show she needn't be so greedy.

"What a house!" Mrs Gamble declared, her long, narrow fingers clasping a mug of the best Java coffee. Filtered, not percolated.

"Yes. Quite a mansion, isn't it? Strange thing

about a big house – you imagine you'll have more space but somehow you don't. You adjust to the proportions."

Besides, space is a preoccupation of the soul. But I didn't feel Mrs Gamble would appreciate my mystic insights. She was still at Hertzberg's "hygiene level" where food on the table was the biggest chore of the day.

Her eyes narrowed as she looked at me.

"Irish, aren't you?" Her tone was accusing rather than enquiring. I was glad she felt there was some way in which she could feel good about being Mrs Gamble.

"Yes. There is some mixed blood somewhere along the line – an Englishman. But we try not to dwell on it."

I hoped that would be the end of the "top dog" game. My hounds could be twice as fierce as anyone else's. I learnt a lot on my mother's knee.

Flora was drawing patterns from the spilt milk with her fingers. Tiny black eyes outlined with long lashes looked on the world with sadness and disappointment.

As if reading my thoughts, her mother volunteered: "Flora misses 'er dad. Haven't heard hide or hair of him since. Must have met a Muslin. They say men go mad for them."

"The unfamiliar often attracts some people;

sultry looks have their charm, especially when you can't understand a word the other person is saying."

She gave me a queer look. With her elbow she stopped Flora drawing with her spilt milk.

"We don't mean to be ungrateful or anything Mrs Ransome but . . ."

She seemed worried, frightened almost. "I think I'd better go back home. We've managed before."

"Nonsense, you can't go back to the cold and the damp mouldy walls. You can spend the night here and we can organise someone to fix up your house."

I got busy with hot water bottles and, inspired, went to the cocktail cabinet – not for the single malt, but for a less exalted whisky. I made up a strong nightcap for both of us. Flora settled for a Coke.

Mrs Gamble had it down in double quick time, was sucking the lemon studded with cloves when Gerald walked into the kitchen.

"Philippa! A party? Have you any idea what time it is?"

I laughed.

"It's no party, Gerald. Poor Mrs Gamble and Flora were going to have to sleep in a cold, damp cottage without any supper and with a bin full of worms that were busy dying."

His look said something like "So what!" but I

pretended not to notice. I distinctly heard him say "for better or worse" on that glorious day in September. He tightened the belt on his cream silk dressing-gown. I felt he probably had nothing on beneath but I did my best not to think about that.

He took in a deep breath and said: "The blue room is aired and cosy – it's just above the kitchen, so it's always warm. I tried to get Philippa to appropriate it but she said that blue reminded her of death."

He gave me a rather piercing look.

"What a good idea! I never thought of the blue room," I said, gathering hot water bottles and ushering the guests out of the kitchen and up the stairs.

I knew Gerald would save the day. I could have done with him years ago.

Within days we were on intimate terms. Gone were "Mrs Ransome this and Mrs Gamble that." It was all "Philippa" and "Letty".

Letty confided that she really didn't like worms:

"It's their cold, wet bodies that squirm and squirm begging you to let them go."

I know the feeling but I never give into it.

"Just try to remember, Letty, that's just their way of moving about, like a baby learning to crawl squirms and wriggles."

Nothing like something practical to give the mind something else to think about.

"Truth is, Philippa, I just don't like worms. I don't even like dogs or cats or budgies. I'm not sure I even like men."

Now that was serious.

"Have you thought of therapy?"

She gave me one of her queer looks but I forged ahead, regardless.

"It can really help you sort out those odd feelings of yours, help you to see another side to life."

She moved away from me and began to dry the dishes with energy.

"Can't say as how I feel I need to sort anything out, as you put it. Therapy is for folk who are gone in the head, like Mags Bideford as was in the post office. She were drinking tea out of her shoes before they got her inside!"

"Perhaps she was practising for Cinderella – there's always a perfectly plausible explanation for people's idiosyncrasies."

We put the dishes away and put the casserole on the Aga for the evening meal. Flora was busily drawing feverishly.

"I think you misunderstand, Letty. Therapy works much better if you're halfway normal to begin with. It's wasted on nutters, they give the whole head-shrinking business a bad name."

When I turned from the cooker she was gone. Flora had the Aga open and was busily stuffing her drawing into the flames. I really was getting too involved. Perhaps Letty needed something practical to keep her mind occupied. With Christmas wending its merry way towards us, she could busy herself with puddings and cakes – *Woodleigh Confections*. She might even make enough money to get Flora a set of colouring pencils.

"I hardly ever see you these days," Gerald said, climbing into bed. "Letty and Flora taking up your time? Really, Philippa you're too full of the milk of human kindness. You mustn't let people take advantage of you. If you ask me Letty and Flora could buy and sell you twice over."

I thought it better to say nothing. Gerald can be a bit cynical at times. Comes from having a family like his. While his mind may be slightly out of kilter, there was absolutely nothing wrong with his body. Oh, how every sinew, muscle and blood vessel moved to perfection.

"Perhaps we'll need to introduce some variations into the main theme, or we'll stagnate like an old married couple. A chandelier might be interesting, for instance. You could perhaps swing . . ." I suggested afterwards.

"That'll do, Philippa. You'll just have to settle for an anglepoise – like any normal person," he said as he turned over.

Who was it said romance dies with the wedding bouquet?

Chapter Seven

Letty set to with amazing alacrity, soaking fruit in brandy, making enormous slabs of marzipan icing. Even tiny Flora put aside her creative scribbles to chop some cherries, though at a snail's pace. I always use the least processed of everything. Ready chopped nuts and fruit make a totally tasteless cake.

At the end of a week we had fifty puddings, neatly wrapped in silver paper and tied with green ribbons. At the end of two weeks we had twenty cakes and forty jars of mincemeat. They were placed under lock and key in the cellars, far from sticky fingers and saboteurs.

Pimmsy was tickled with it all. "Mad buggers" he exclaimed every time he wandered in for a cup of tea.

"What on earth do we need all these for?" he asked.

"To give Letty and Flora some money for

Christmas. We'll sell them through *Woodleigh Enterprises*."

He seemed slightly sceptical.

"Don't worry," I reassured, "there won't be one left by Christmas Eve."

The man thought I was an idiot.

It seemed that Woodleigh Hall traditionally feasted on goose at Christmas. Letty said she knew "a woman on the way to Norwich who kept them on grass and fed them organic grain."

I never kept geese – they can be terrifying and are reputed to be able to break arms. In some parts of the world they are still kept as guards, more effective than rotweillers but better eating.

We got to Stratton Strawless and took a narrow road in the middle of the village which led us to the Goose Lady's cottage. She came to the door brandishing a saucepan.

"I thought it were some of them kids from the village. They don't half make my life a misery with their thieving ways and cheek. Not like long ago when the worst we did was pinch apples from Lockinge Hall down the road."

"We've come for a goose, Mrs . . . Em," I said taking a deep breath. Dealing with country folk can be tricky. "I heard yours were the best available." I attempted flattery.

"Not only the best – the only ones reared

properly," she corrected me. "Nowt but the best of grain and grass. Cossetted and coddled. Makes the flesh tender, see. Miserable animals only make tough eating. Same with people, I expect. But I prefer goose. Nicer habits."

She took an oilcloth apron from a hook inside the door, pulled it over her head and tied it firmly around her waist.

"They'll be out in the hedgerows this time of year, picking the falling berries, eating any green shoot that pokes its head out."

We marched in single file behind her, along a tiny cobbled path that led through a walled garden and into a meadow beyond. Gigantic geese filled the field, undulating like white horses on the sea. As soon as they saw their mistress, they stretched their necks and foamed forward. Letty and I looked at each other and made a beeline for the garden wall.

"Soon as they see they're wasting their time, they'll go back," Mrs Goose shouted above the din. We were not convinced and watched from our stone perch.

"Look how she loves them," Letty said through chattering teeth. Sure enough, Goose Person was patting some and caressing others, uttering an encouraging word here, an admonishment there. I hadn't realised there was much room in a goose's head for such a brain, able to recognise affection. But then, look at the size of the Pentium chip.

Out of her pocket GP took a handful of grain and, circling around the geese, looking and examining, held it to one in particular. It took the bait as gently as a baby and followed her for more. In the split second when she was leading it, and the others hadn't worked out that food was in the offing, she swung to one side of it, grabbed its neck and stood with her foot on it.

"Oh God," Letty said. "What a cruel woman. One minute she's feeding it and the next she's choking it. Put you off goose for life."

"Makes you respect animals a bit more perhaps and be grateful for what we eat."

"Why can't we all just eat beans?"

"For the very reason you don't, Letty. We seem to need variety in our food and all sorts of minerals and vitamins. Anyway, a dish of beans would make eating a very dull business."

Mrs Goose brought the limp body to us.

"Another week and that poor goose would have been too fat to get about," she said, running her fingers along its silky neck. "It died out in the fresh air on a full belly. Hope the rest of us have as pleasant an end."

Letty put out a shaking hand towards the white shape.

"Must keep those lovely feathers for a cushion and make a good job of cooking it. Though it *is* a pity they can't just live."

"That's what I say to Ben, my husband," she replied. "I miss them when they've all gone. But at least they're not force-fed to make that *pâté* stuff like them Frenchies do. That's what I call cruel." She wrapped her huge hands with their sausage-like fingers around the body. "Come in and we'll have a nice cup of tea and I'll tell you how to cook it for the best."

We trundled back to the cottage and sat on rush-work chairs in front of an open fire. Bowing to modernity, Mrs G stretched towards the latest fan oven and whipped out a tray of scones.

As if reading my mind, she said: "Better'n any range. Same result every time. No worries about putting on enough fuel or too much. Present from Ben."

"Are the geese your only produce on the farm, Mrs . . . ?" I enquired.

"There's a few acres of raspberries and strawberries and Ben has his herb business in the outhouse. Nettle water for rheumatism. Keeps him busy. Folk find it a godsend."

As we said our farewells, with goosey gander in a plastic bag under my arms, a shining new Volvo Estate purred up to the door. Ben. By the looks of it, there was a penny or two in nettle juice.

He nodded at us, a handsome man in a tweed suit, looking as if he ought to be ascending a flight of marble stairs rather than entering a humble cottage.

"Tax avoidance," Letty explained, as she got into the car beside me. "No point in him buying a big fancy house. He'd lose it all. Only way to get rich in this life is to inherit it or win the pools."

She crossed her arms and wore her ill-done-to expression.

"You're all right, though," she said, casting one of her sidelong glances at me. "The third way to get rich is to marry into money."

It had been the last thing on my mind but Letty wouldn't understand that.

"Surely that option is open to you too, Letty?"

"Who'd take on someone else's brat, unless the woman had fantastic good looks or big boobs."

Letty can be rudimentary at times. Her way of letting off steam about life.

"You have lots of good qualities," I said in an attempt to console, though I felt I should keep quiet.

"That's damning with faint praise. I'm good in parts, like the curate's egg, is that it?"

I put my foot on the accelerator and turned up the radio a titch. Even *I* have feelings.

The goose was still warm when we laid it on the kitchen table, so we set to plucking it before the feathers anchored themselves in the pool of cooling wax at their base. After two hours the bird had a nice smooth chest and legs like a film star; however its wings were a mass of pin feathers.

"Afraid it's a job for a pliers, Letty and for tougher arms than either of us."

Gerald refused to cooperate.

"Can't stand the smell of plucked feathers," he said, just like that!

"I'm sure you'll want to eat the thing, all the same."

This reached something in him.

"I suppose I could do with a cup of coffee," he said following me down the tiny staircase.

I hoped his readers didn't need to keep themselves as wide awake reading his books as he seemed to need to do in order to write them.

Gerald looked at the heap of white feathers on the floor and the pieces of down which hadn't yet landed, not to mention the ones Flora was putting in her mouth.

"Get those feathers out of that child's mouth. She could pick up anything," he said. "Philippa, why on earth couldn't you have bought one ready-plucked and eviscerated from the supermarket. There's no need to be a martyr."

I waved the pliers about in a threatening manner. Letty and Flora disappeared into the pantry.

"For a start, Gerald dear, a supermarket goose wouldn't have anything like the flavour of this fellow who just a few hours ago was gadding about in the open air, eating grain and grass. The supermarket one was probably fed with pellets made from chicken factory refuse."

He gave me one of his mother superior looks.

"Give me those pliers, Philippa. You obviously have never plucked a goose before."

True but I admitted to nothing.

He took the pliers and, kneeling before the bird, deftly removed the remaining pin feathers with sharp tugs and a practised flick of the wrist I had never seen before. He continued to astonish me with his mastery of elemental things.

"Gerald," I asked in my little red riding hood voice, "where on earth did you learn such deft movements?"

"A few short months married and she's already forgotten who I am. Well, Pips, if you don't remember, I'm certainly too hurt and upset to remind you."

I racked my brain and tried not to get angry at being called "Pips".

"Africa?" I asked, suddenly remembering the panache with which he drove my tractor.

"Well . . . I suppose I'll forgive you – just this once."

He got up and gave me a strong, hard kiss on the lips.

What a waste of a good man to the world of writing. He should spend all his time with me; I would be such a good person then.

"You ought to join in the daily doings more often," I said leaning towards him in a more neighbourly fashion.

"At the rate the money is pouring out of this place, we need every penny we can lay our hands on."

"Are things as bad as that? Why don't you tell me about it?"

"Yes. I am. The harvests have been very poor and make a loss each year. Multiply that by five and you can imagine the deficit."

"Why not rent, or lease the land?"

"Because the place is too much in debt. These things are OK if you want to tick over. We need cash – and fast. Remember your free range chicken idea? I'm due a few royalties; we could buy a few hundred birds."

Is that why he married me – to save Woodleigh? I didn't dare ask, it would spoil my depression.

"Also, I've another book finished and the bones of a further one for after Christmas."

"Perhaps you're working too hard, Gerald. Now might be a good time to take a break, perhaps visit London . . ."

"You know we can't both be away, Philippa. Remember your strawberries? All too easy for Mortimer to blame someone else for his own wrongdoing when we're not here to keep an eye out."

I meant Mortido's horse no harm but I did wish it would slip and throw its rider – nothing serious, just a slight paralysis from the neck down. But I mentally spanked myself for such wicked thoughts. All the same . . .

"But Letty's here now. And I could ask the Goodhews to keep an eye out for anything suspicious, riders on horseback, Pimmsied old men."

"Maybe – yes, perhaps a weekend. He couldn't get up to too much mischief in one weekend?"

I was already deciding where to stay, where to visit and what to bring.

Coincidentally, Canon Goodhew sent one of his curt notes: "Dates for Diary: Fri: Last meeting of year of Woodleigh Enterprises. Sat: Christmas Sale. Rgds, S."

"We must bring some of our goodies to the meeting, Letty. Then, once word gets around, they'll sell like hotcakes."

I could see she didn't believe a word of it. Letty has only known failure, a feeling that's very hard to shift.

Speaking of which, Agatha's letter still lay unopened. Screwing my courage, and armed with a glassful of vintage port, I braved its contents.

Dear Philippa – it sounded bad already; she doesn't use formalities for nothing.

Even though you're married you still have a first

family you know. Eddie said you weren't the sort to forget that, but I just thought I'd mention it anyway. I've had another bout of depression. They were good to me in the hospital but, really, there are so many sick people out there, I decided to let them have the bed. Life is so cruel and so hard. Eddie says it's still no reason for me to destroy myself with drink. We'd a terrible row about it. He just doesn't understand that if I didn't relax with a drink, I may as well throw in the towel. He keeps insisting on me seeing a shrink but honestly, I know more than they do about the workings of the human mind. Therapy is for nutcases. Apart from the expense. And to think that all this is just because I was born at the wrong time for Mummy.

I hadn't the heart to read any further. Aggie's level of awareness was arrested at the amoeba stage. She'd no intention of making her way to shore and taking a look around.

I tore up the letter and watched it burn to nothing.

"Philippa! Haven't seen you for an age," Gladys said, grabbing both my hands and pulling me into the room. "We've a visitor this evening," she nodded towards a small man, whose shrunken face indicated a drug problem – nicotine, alcohol or ecstasy, perhaps all three. "He's from the rural development commission. Wants to offer us a whole lot of money in grants to develop enterprise in the county." Gladys was flushed with excitement.

I smelt a rat. There is no such thing as a free grant. Simon was busy smiling at him and being his most unctuous. A grave mistake.

Letty had the long table covered with a white cloth and was busy arranging her Christmas fare. She certainly had an eye for marketing, if only she'd be a bit more cheerful about life. It was a day's work to keep her spirits up.

Inexorably, Gladys led me to Mr Wonderful. He looked up at me with ferrety eyes.

"Heard so much about you. You've been the inspiration to Woodleigh. It's people like you we want to encourage."

Indeed. Just so that they can fill your quota to produce a few hundred jobs a year.

"I'm not sure how you can help," I said mildly. "We're merely fledglings, at this stage. Finding our feet."

"Just the sort of venture we're actively seeking." He smiled through his teeth. Nicotine certainly.

"I'm not sure, at this stage, whether we need capital. We're keeping the investment as low as possible."

"Don't worry about that – we have start-up grants, grants for feasibility studies and grants for capital investment, like machinery and buildings."

"All, no doubt, needing some percentage from our side."

"Well, of course, people should put their money where their mouth is. If they really believe in something, they would be prepared to mortgage their house, take out a bank loan, sell the family heirlooms and follow it through to the end."

"Sometimes that is exactly where things finish."

"Oh, don't mind our Pippy," the Canon rushed in, "she can be very strong about things."

Especially when I see stupidity.

Gladys called the meeting to order, interrupting several sales of cakes. Letty's face was flushed with pleasure at seeing her stack of goods diminish.

"We're very pleased to introduce Mr Hazlett to our little group. Mr Hazlett is here to chat to us about how he can be of help in making our little venture with worms and compost and such-like grow."

A feeble clap preceded Mr Hazlett's progress to the centre of the stage.

"And a very good evening to you all. We've been keeping a watchful eye on proceedings in Woodleigh and so far . . . we like what we see. Though, I hasten to add, you have a lot to learn." He paused to wiggle his tie. "But that is where the rural development commission comes in. We provide the expertise, advice on finance, machinery, computers, markets, etc. so that your venture is a success."

"Are you saying we couldn't do that without you?" I couldn't resist enquiring – which is exactly what he was insinuating.

"If you'll just let me finish, I'll explain what I mean. Thank you."

He fumbled in his pocket and extracted a long thin cigar that looked as if it had been languishing in the lining for just such an emergency.

"You are the people who know your product, who provide the enthusiasm. Look on us as Father Christmas who provides the little sacks of gold at the right time to keep you producing, growing and making money."

"Do we have to give your little bags of gold back?" It was the thin man who grudged the money for a worm bin.

"A lot of it is EU money, so they won't be asking for it back." He laughed at this, thinking it a great joke. "All you have to do is keep an account of what happened to it and follow the rule book about how it is to be spent."

There was a dangerous hum of agreement and enthusiasm from those who were still awake. Who could blame them? The man was more or less offering them a blank cheque. Little did they realise it would be the end of everything, that nothing kills motivation faster than unearned income and uninformed interference. How to let them know without sounding as if I had a vested interest in attaching everything to myself was the tricky bit. When in doubt, do nothing.

We were shown graphs, cash flow projections, types of factory, marketing strategies and the use of computers. Of course everyone was impressed. Mr Hazlett lit another cigar in celebration. Gladys went to put the kettle on. Woodleigh was going to be the boom village of the century.

There was only one dissenting voice. Mr Manifold got to his feet, eventually, and said: "Summat wrong here. Must be a catch somewhere. No such thing as a free lunch, in my opinion."

Of course everyone laughed and pooh-poohed and Mr Manifold sat down heavily.

The charts and headings were put away and the biscuits taken out. Mr Hazlett pinched all the chocolate ones. I refused the jam hearts and café noirs.

"Well, what do you think, Pips?" the Canon whispered behind me.

"Do you really want me to tell you?"

He came around to face me.

"You mean you are not impressed, Philippa?"

"In a nutshell, no. The rural development commission are simply laundering taxpayer's money. They don't give a tuppenny damn what happens to it, so long as they can say to their committee that X thousands of pounds was handed out, creating X number of jobs. When things go wrong, as inevitably they do, they have someone to blame – in this case *Woodleigh Enterprises*.

"Why do you say 'inevitably'?"

"Businesses don't grow just because you throw money at them! They grow because someone else wants what you produce and is willing to buy it again and again. No amount of money will make it a success."

"That's not the case with *Woodleigh Enterprises*, though – is it?"

"The whole point is at this moment we do not know. We're merely experimenting. It's completely the wrong time to put money into a business. When we're sure the demand is there, some cash is very useful to hurry up the production process. But as little as possible. What people tend to do is buy expensive factory buildings and machinery, pay for expensive expertise like creative accountants, marketing whizz-kids and designers. Before you know where you are you've spent a fortune without even producing one bag of compost."

"I understand your logic but how do you *know* all this to be true?"

I'd met with that reaction before. Was it because I was a woman? Because I seemed so sure of myself? I simply looked at the Canon and decided no amount of sense could penetrate his boyish enthusiasm. Any dissension would be interpreted as being a "dampner."

"A bit negative tonight, are we?" he asked.

I glanced at Letty to see if she was ready to come home. Three cakes left. Better to leave her to sell everything. One in the eye for Pimmsy.

"I'm going, Simon. Would you be kind enough to drop Letty off?"

I didn't bother waiting for an answer but went to pour the undrinkable tea down the sink.

"You're not going so soon, Philippa!" Gladys stopped me on the way to the kitchen.

"If I stay, I may say something I'll regret," I said, rinsing my cup.

"But you may be entitled to a nice fat salary if you're in charge of the whole business."

"I've no intention of wasting money needlessly, Gladys; I'm happy to give my time freely. Don't forget that money has to come from somewhere. If it's wasted and not used to create more, then it leaves a hole wherever it came from. It's not a bottomless pit. At this rate the EU will be bankrupt in next to no time."

She looked thoughtfully at me. There was a glimmer of understanding.

"But that won't happen in Woodleigh."

Famous last words.

"But you'll miss getting a computer, Philippa."

"If you read between the lines, Gladys, you'd have noticed that the computers we're being offered are very expensive – twice the price of any other computer in fact. And we must buy this particular one and fork out half the money ourselves. Let me tell you Gladys, that for half the money you could go into any shop and buy exactly the same computer."

"But that's disgraceful! Some company is obviously lining its pockets."

She was beginning to see the light. But would she pull back the curtain fully?

The journey home seemed interminable. I could barely wait for intelligent company, someone to agree with me.

Gerald was reading a print-out of his latest creation, a steaming mug of coffee and the radio on full blast.

"How on earth can you concentrate with all of that going on?" I nodded towards the mug and radio.

"Helps to fill the void while you're not by my side. How did it go?"

"I think my involvement with *Woodleigh Enterprises* ended tonight. Unless they come to their senses."

He put down the manuscript and heaved his manly chest upright.

"That's hard luck, Philippa. All the work you put into it too. Nothing to be salvaged?"

"Not a thing. They wouldn't listen. All they see

are pound notes. They don't think, though maybe one or two of them might. Story of my life. I see too much. It's a lonely old station."

"One can never see too much, Philippa. *Illegitimis noncarborundum*. Tell them what you think."

"I tried. All they do is fling rubbish at the messenger. Better to finish now than have even greater heartbreak later."

Not to mention all that money on my conscience.

"Besides, the free range chickens will probably need my undivided attention. And there's our weekend in London."

I leaned across him and helped myself to his mug of coffee.

"You should do that more often, Pips," he said, putting a hand on my back, preventing me from getting up.

I put the mug down and turned around. We demonstrated how much we missed each other. As the World Service came on, it was time to turn out the lights.

Where would we be without life's little pick-me-ups?

On the morning we left for London my nose was streaming and my eyes burned in my head. Too much gardening in damp weather with Stoat, who seemed to be immune to anything, had given me a cold.

"Rain softens the hair," he said in the middle of a downpour, still earthing up the strawberry plants while I took refuge under an overhang of ivy. He had taken off his hat to let the rain drip its way through his dense mop of hair. Probably the only time it saw any sort of water. He winked at me as if hearing the thought.

I asked him to keep an "eye out" while we were in London.

"If you happen to be around that is," I added, knowing he likes his weekends to himself.

"He won't touch them strawberries again, that's for sure," he said. "Nor nothing else, while I'm around. You enjoy yourself, Mrs Gerald."

Which I had every intention of doing but the cold wind and stuffed nose and head were militating against it. By the time we reached Piccadilly Circus I'd gone through a box of tissues and tied my hair back in irritation. Nothing worse than hair sitting on your neck when you're feeling poorly.

Gerald was silent as he negotiated the traffic, tension showing in the whiteness of his knuckles on the steering wheel.

"Couldn't we just park and use the tube?" I asked.

"What on earth do you think I'm trying to do?

Do you really think I'm whizzing around here with my life in my hands just for the hell of it?"

Ask a stupid question . . .

We stopped eventually and limp with perspiration and a temperature, I dragged myself from the car.

"I need a cup of tea," I said. "Would you like to join me or shall we meet later?"

"I like that! We come all the way to London and you can't wait to get rid of me!"

I wasn't sure whether I did or not, so I said nothing. He walked beside me nonetheless as I made my way to the National Gallery and descended to the restaurant.

"I thought you were going to do some shopping?" Gerald quizzed me.

"All in good time," I mumbled between wet tissues, gratefully sipping the hot tea and allowing it to melt over a very inferior, though welcome, chocolate brownie. Everyone makes the mistake of using cheap chocolate in brownies. It simply doesn't work.

Gerald was silent, munching an oat cake and drinking coffee. I looked through the list of paintings I wanted to see and hoped they were all around and not at the menders or rolled up in some thief's drawer.

"Sorry, Pippy." Gerald leaned towards me. I loved him when he apologised. It made me feel nothing was my fault, when, try as I may, I still experienced a smidgen of guilt for no reason. Legacy of a punitive upbringing.

"Don't worry. Forgiveness is my middle name. All that driving must have taken it out of you."

"Maybe. I suppose I was frightened we'd die or something, just when I was feeling happier than I've ever felt in my life."

Two minds with but a single . . . Marriage not only removes your name and independence but allows your mind to be taken over too. I couldn't think of a nicer person to do it.

I squeezed his hand. "Let's go and see a few paintings."

Half the world had a similar idea. Small, but perfectly formed, Japanese tourists clustered at certain paintings – the Piero, the Leonardo cartoon and of course the Van Gogh – as if these had received some imprimatur. It was all right to even like them.

"What on earth is all the fuss about?" Gerald asked.

Of course Gerald is a "word" person, not in the least visual.

"Well, it is a Leonardo – though of course that doesn't mean it's a good painting. You must admit, though, it does capture a likeness."

"Certainly. It makes drawing look easy – just like my books make writing look like falling off a log. I like to think so anyway," he said a little defensively.

"I think you're books are wonderful, Gerald." I attempted the usual female thing of soothing the injured ego. Where do we get it from? Perhaps it wasn't a "female" thing at all, just the usual humane way of chucking a fellow human under the chin.

It wasn't till we reached the Piero that he dropped his bombshell.

"Philippa . . . ," he continued to stare at the *Resurrection*, "I must confess, Pippy, that I've been feeling very aggrieved that you still haven't bothered to read any of my books."

There wasn't a seat in sight. The brownies were about to declare a revolution. I wanted to say of all the cheek to expect me to sit reading your computer outpourings as well as run an estate, defend it against the depredations of your brother and father and the ravings of your crazy sister!

But I kept my lips sealed. The nuns would have been so pleased. Martyrdom is the highest accolade.

"Did you hear what I said, Philippa?"

"I heard you perfectly well. I'm not sure I completely understand, however. I feel I'm being whacked on the knuckles for not doing something I simply haven't had the time to do."

"That's my point. You're not really interested. You couldn't care less about something that occupies 80% of my time."

"That's precisely my objection to your writing, Gerald. If you must know. It overtakes you. Your every thought is on it, every breath you take, every sigh that issues from your delicate lips is directly related to it."

Where do I fit in? I wanted to ask, but that would seem like begging.

The Piero had vanished, like so many of the other paintings, in a blur. We were before the Arnolfini portrait. One of my favourites.

As if taken by the picture, Gerald held my hand even more tightly. Two people betrothed, Giovanni proudly showing his Giovanna in a state of late pregnancy.

"Was she pregnant before the marriage?" Gerald asked.

"Of course," I replied.

What better reason to get married than to have children? The rest is masochism.

I wondered about the Arnolfini baby, its proud parents looking forward to its arrival. Wanting it. Loving it. How I envied them.

"Let's go and get you a decent lunch, Pips. You don't look very happy."

The lunch, Italian with home made pasta, a thick tomato sauce heavy with basil and a cherry-like Chianti, failed to lift me. It could have been sawdust and ink. Strange how our taste buds go on strike just when we need to be cheered up.

"How about a truffle?"

I could barely shake my head.

"Not even a truffle can wash away poor Pippy's tears? Am I a terrible old ogre?"

The mother hen in me was roused to defend the weak. The heraldic symbol of Woodcock is a Pelican feeding her young with the flesh from her own breast.

"No. Gerald. You're not an ogre. You want your writing appreciated and what could be fairer? It's important to you. I just feel I can do nothing right."

"What would you like – for you?"

I knew it almost before he had finished the question. But I didn't dare admit it. "A good question," I said. "A good question."

Gerald's editor was to call at our hotel in the afternoon.

"I'm happy for you to join us, though it will probably be a bit boring."

I was determined to show more interest in my husband's career.

"I'd be delighted to."

I opened the door to someone who seemed young enough to be my daughter.

Gerald introduced "Ruthie". Indeed.

I played hostess, pouring coffee and just the right amount of milk and several heaped teaspoons of sugar.

We sat down and pretended it was going to be fun.

"Well, Gerald your latest offering needs one or two major changes – I didn't like the character of Mrs Beasley. She seems to me to be a formidable sort of woman, full of spunk, unlikely to put up with the snivellings of her weedy husband. I'd like you either to tone her down or give her husband a bit of oomph. It just doesn't work as it is."

To emphasise what an expert on everything she was, Ruthless spread her leg to reveal more shiny black stocking top and bent forward to give an itsy, bitsy peek of the little pears that were popping from the top of her dress.

Gerald had become alarmingly pale. He had that faraway look in his eye, the one that carried him to the Elysian fields of his mind, away from pain. I could cheerfully have laddered her tights.

"Now the second major change is the way the plot moves from the scene of the murder to the mind of murderer and back again. As a device it's a bit too cutesy, a bit *tiré par les cheveux* as the Frogs say. I think it would be much better to concentrate on one or the other."

Gerald wasn't listening. I tried to give her my best impression of a head mistress. She stared defiantly back.

"Apart from that, it's a terrific book. By far the best you've written. The characterisation, with of course a few minor changes here and there, works very well. Once the plot has been straightened out, it'll be a humdinger."

Perhaps I could jump up quickly and spill the remains of the coffee over the velvet bows on her shoes . . .

Gerald still hadn't come to.

"How many writers are you, em, working with at the moment?" I really wanted to say "torturing."

"Oh, too many. They're all so temperamental! Present company excepted, of course! Writers tend to be absolutely egocentric. Can't bear you to criticise their work."

"I imagine it's quite difficult for them, all that work, alone."

"Just because it's hard doesn't mean it's perfect!" she snapped.

Would she know perfection if she saw it?

Gerald was drinking cold coffee and staring into space.

"Well, I'd better get going. Another call to make."

Ruthless stood up and pulled her skirt two inches below her bottom, gathering her wits before her next onslaught. She had rather nice legs and a pretty face when she smiled.

"Do you do any writing yourself?" I asked.

"My mother always said I'd be useless at it."

Hell hath no fury like a writer *manqué*.

"Don't bother. I'll see myself out."

"Gerald!" I found myself squeaking when I heard the lift doors close. "How on earth can you bear to have someone treat you like that? She looks far too young to have gotten through reading Dickens let alone anyone else."

"I know," he said feebly.

"How can you put up with it? Sounds like you have to re-write the whole book."

"Just about."

Gerald's gloom settled on me and gathered blackness like a runaway snowball gathers snow. Not even the walk along the Thames, the visit to a wine bar or the champagne supper Gerald had ordered at *Restaurant Pierre* raised a flicker of cheer. I was dead inside, my heart cold, the pictures in my head black. Not helped by feeling guilty that I ought to be enjoying myself.

"Don't worry, Gerald. We'll get onto these chickens, make a fortune, buy our house in the South of France and retire there for six months of the year."

The poor man looked at me hopefully. In that instant I felt responsible for our happiness. Not a nice feeling. I needed looking after too.

That evening our lovemaking began with a sort of desperation and ended with an exhaustion born of low spirits. We stayed clasped to each other until dawn broke.

"Some fresh air today, Philippa? That cold of yours sounds worse."

"My snoring keep you awake?" My throat was raw from breathing through my mouth.

"Not at all. It transported me back to my childhood and my hidey-hole above the hogs' shed."

I did something unspeakable under the bedclothes.

"Really Philippa! You certainly know how to get to a man. Unfortunately, all that rough stuff merely inflames me."

The slight, though meaningful delay forced us to abandon a complete tour of Kew and do a cursory one instead. Just as well. I was bored after ten minutes.

"Thought you liked gardens!"

"Yes, when they don't look like a giant field with trees dotted here and there. It's all too clinical, like a trial plot."

And the herbaceous borders were a mockery of the genre, even at this time of year. A few gypsophila and delphinium and that was that.

"Perhaps it's the mood you're in. They say we project whatever we're feeling onto the world outside ourselves, that certain people select particular flowers and thus express the unconscious side to their nature."

"What if you have a passion for red hot pokers?"

"If you were to ask me, I'd say someone like that can't think of anything beyond the phallus. They're probably reasonably happily married with an excellent lover for a husband but they can never have enough."

Fortunately, there isn't a single red hot poker on my little farm.

"In fact," Gerald hadn't quite finished, "someone like that wouldn't have a single red hot poker near them for fear of giving the game away."

I stared at the ground.

"Still anxious to visit this goatperson of yours on the way home?" He slipped an arm through mine.

"Yes. Perhaps something can be salvaged from the day."

I was cross at having my hidden shallows detected, even by Gerald.

The European expert on matters caprine lived in Beech Lane, outside Saxmundham. Her home was a prefabricated bungalow in the middle of a row of similar dwellings. A long meadow stretched at the back, enclosed by chestnut paling. A white head with horns scratched itself on a doorpost.

"You often mention owners growing to look like their animals but that's taking it a bit far."

"Perhaps you ought to try writing mystery stories with a comic twist – you know, *Goatprints in the Sand, Hey waiter there's a horn in my Soup*, that sort of thing. Cheer Ruthie up no end."

"Perhaps you'd like to visit Madame Goat on your own?"

I planted a wet kiss on his soft lips. It did the trick.

We went around the back of the bungalow, setting off the cairn terrier next door. A thick fog rose from a dung heap as we turned into the yard. The scratching goat let out a whicker.

"We've been announced," Gerald said, searching for signs of human life.

"'Arf a mo," a voice from somewhere shouted. A clash of buckets announced the Goatlady of Saxmundham. Milk slopped onto the path as she made her way towards us. She put down her buckets and cradled my hands in an enormous sea of flesh with sausage-like projections. Milking clearly develops all the tiny muscles most of us will never meet.

I introduced ourselves. Gerald was enchanted. His eyes took on writer's glaze. I sensed the germination of *The Mystery of the Murdered Goat*.

"Writer aren't you?" she queried.

"Yes. Actually. You've perhaps read . . ."

I sensed Gerald's quickening pulse, preparation for adulation.

"No. Never 'eard of you in library. It was Mrs Ransome told me you was a writer – just like me!" She took up her buckets again and led us towards the house.

I hadn't the heart to look at Gerald.

"Kettle'll be boiled," she reassured. There was a protesting whicker from the itchy goat. "You'll get yours later!" she shouted. "Jealous they get if they see anyone come in. Delays their treats."

"They sound almost human," I said trying to make conversation.

She looked at me. "Better'n *some* so-called humans, I can tell ye."

I would have to watch my step.

Every square inch of wall was covered with goatlore – goats with winning trophies, goats with kids, goats chomping hay; some had the goatperson alongside, a large hand holding onto a goat halter for dear life. Above a doorway, the light caught the glass eye of a goat head, mounted on wood.

"My first Billy," Goatina informed. Gerald's eyes were now double-glazed. I shuddered to think what he was making of the sawn off head.

With her giant ham-like hands, she lifted an enormous cast iron frying pan, the sort that was used to heat beans for soldiers in the Crimea. Gerald slipped out of his reverie and leapt forward to help. Naturally she was delighted. "Thank you ever so much," she said, in a sidelong, nanny-like simper. "We'll have some drop scones in a jiffy. If you wouldn't mind heating up teapot." She pointed to a blue enamelled pot roasting itself on the range.

The first of the scones were before me, closely

followed by goat butter and fresh cream. Gerald nudged me and nodded at the raspberry jam. He gave me one of those "Go on, enjoy yourself looks." I always obey my husband, so I put a knob of butter in the middle, a dollop of cream, a spoonful of jam and opened my mouth wide.

From the blue teapot Gerald poured light brown tea.

"Come on now, Miss Hillier, enough slaving away over a hot pan," Gerald said, and made room at the table. She sat as far away from me as possible.

"Philippa was telling me about your latest tome, *The Dairy Goat*."

A nod was as good as a wink. She took two books from an enormous stack in the broom cupboard and gave us one each. Not bad for a first draft and the photographs were good.

"The proceeds go back into the goats. Don't feel you've to buy one," she wiped her nose. A gentleman to the core, Gerald reached for his wallet and paid for both. I could always give one to Sophia, as a Christmas present.

"You said in your letter, Mrs Ransome, as how you wanted to set up a goat dairy."

"Indeed," I replied. It had seemed like a good idea at the time. "However, I wasn't too sure if I could stomach the smell of a few dozen goats in an enclosed space."

"Smell!" she bridled. "Goats don't *smell*. Worse smell of all is humans."

"Well, I can't honestly say I've tried milking any of those!" I helped myself to another drop-scone. Beautiful the way the butter slides around, the cream on top melts like the bottom of a glacier and the jam weighs the whole thing down.

Everything seemed suddenly quiet. Gerald wasn't breathing. Goatina was staring into her teacup, a cold drop scone on her plate.

"Very good scones," I said to the silence.

Goatina looked up. I'd obviously put my foot in it somewhere. Sometimes I don't give myself credit for people paying attention to what I have to say.

"In fact, I had one goat. Nanny," I said, making a gigantic effort to be pleasant. "She died last year, just after giving birth to twins. It felt like losing my best friend. Goats are so *sympathique*."

"Just what I think! It's the mountain breeding, the fresh air."

Gerald let out a sigh. Whose side is that man on anyway?

Clutching two copies of *The Dairy Goat*, a carton of goat yoghurt, a large pat of the cottage cheese that had been busy dripping in a cheesecloth, and the remainder of the now cold drop-scones, we said our farewells with promises of return visits and watching out for mystery novels.

"That was fun." I put on my seat belt and waved madly once again.

"The woman loves her goats," Gerald said the obvious. "Substitute children, I suppose."

"Some human obviously let her down badly. Could be worse. Might have been pekinese. Of course, there's still hope. Even at sixty it's not out of the question to start a family, though she'd have to do a bit better than *The Dairy Goat* to pay the doctor. Perhaps *Tales of the Saxmundham Goat-herd* would fly off the shelves."

"Philippa, really! Hardly enough in that to fill a page."

"I thought you were the one with imagination. I could think of at least half a dozen exploits he could get up to."

"Let me guess . . . something to do with 'horns' anyway, and spying on lovers in the gorse on a hot summer's day . . . "

How does that man manage to read my mind?

Between Halesworth and Bungay the wind got up. Snow flurries did a kamikaze act on the windscreen.

"Beautiful the way they land and then melt to nothingness," I said, feeling happy with the world after our big feed on chips, fried egg and tomato in Halesworth. Nothing like stodgy food to make you realise how lucky you are not to be addicted to it.

"Just so long as they continue to melt," Gerald said, a slight touch of anxiety in his voice. "Storms can blow up without warning in this part of the world."

A few miles further on, the heater went. Gerald gave it a vicious kick.

"Gerald! What violence! Makes a girl scared."

"She'll be even more scared when I tell her this is one helluva storm we're heading into and no heater."

True enough the flurries got bigger and didn't melt quite so quickly. And me with my Hush Puppy slip-ons. I tried rubbing my feet.

"I daren't stop, Philippa." When he used my baptismal name, I knew it was serious. "Get the newspaper, tear it into strips and line your shoes with them. Then make a little tent for your feet."

"What about you?"

"I'll be OK. I can do the exercises I learnt from the Sherpas. Mainly self-hypnosis: you imagine your feet in a pan of water that's being slowly brought to the boil. You turn the gas off just as the bubbles appear."

Gerald can be comical at times. Half an hour later, my shoes lined and tented but no warmer, we seemed to have been lost in a black tunnel with someone with a warped sense of humour throwing feathers at us. The wipers still worked. Just. Every now and then the snow got too heavy for the blade and it quivered and whined for a few seconds and then shot to the other side of the windscreen. Like the gentleman he was, Gerald was sparing the "little woman" any worry. He needn't have bothered. I could supply my own, infinitely more catastrophic. I tried to keep breathing and wished, for the umpteenth time in a month, that I still smoked.

"Damn! The clutch has gone. All that driving in low gear did for it. Ropey anyway."

"What on earth were you doing going on a long journey with a ropey clutch?" I shrieked, my anxiety getting the better of me.

"We'll have to pull in."

The car ground to a halt. There were no identifiable outlines in the pitch blackness and whirl of snowflakes.

"You're quite right, Pips. It's totally my fault. We'll be OK, I promise. I got down from Everest to tell the tale, after all."

I forbore to tell him of people who have come round the world in a boat single-handed only to be knocked down by a bus on their way home.

"We have a choice. We can stay here, try to stay warm and wait till daybreak. Or we can walk to the nearest town."

I didn't know which was worse.

"Or, I could walk to the nearest town to get help and leave you in the car."

The fear showed in my eyes.

"Flagging down a car is out of the question. Count Dracula might be on the prowl. Nothing for it. We'll walk. Better put another layer of newspaper into your shoes and whatever other crevices you can find."

"What about yourself?"

"Don't worry, Pips, I'm still *pinus intacta*."

I didn't know where to look.

The gale I'd been caught in on my first outing with the college ramblers all those years ago was nothing compared to the power behind the one that greeted us when we opened the car doors. We quickly climbed back in.

"That wasn't much use. We haven't even a torch. And your newspaper is soggy already."

I extricated the cold lumps of *papier maché* and my numbed fingers tore some more strips. The one occasion a mobile phone would be very useful. Such are the punishments meted out to those who buck the trend.

"Shame we don't have a mobile phone," Gerald said, reading my mind again. "Scrabble would be useful, or Trivial Pursuits. Even a travelling domino set would be welcome."

He always had *me* of course.

On cue, he bent towards me. The tip of his tongue brought my lips to life and, fortunately, I was able to respond. Within minutes the steam from my toes dried the rest of the soggy paper and with the tilting of the seat, whatever vestige of propriety that remained within me vanished.

"You know, Pips, if Mike Stroud had brought

you with him to the Antarctic, he wouldn't have lost half of his member."

"Not from frostbite anyway."

As the wind abated and the snow settled for a steady pile up, the traffic stopped and the view beyond the windows became invisible.

"Warmer now because of the layer of snow around the car. We'd probably be warmer in the back seat."

The smell of leather never seemed so sweet. It became warm enough for Gerald to discard the deerstalker, sheepskin gloves and tie pin. Battling with the thermal longjohns was more difficult. Did the manufacturers never hear of velcro?

Several hours later a sliver of sunlight shone on us through the gap between the top of the snow-filled windscreen and the roof of the car.

"Just like the burial chamber at Newgrange in the winter solstice," I remarked to Gerald. "And we don't have to put our names down and be a member of the serious archaeological squad to experience it."

Writer's glaze crept over his face once again.

"A body discovered in the chamber – but not 3,000 years old?" I enquired.

"You'll have to write some of these yourself! No. I was thinking of something else."

"Well, *déculote ta pensée*, you're amongst friends."

"As a matter of fact, I was just thinking what a

lucky man I am, in the back seat of a car with a gorgeous, wonderful person like you."

For the second time in twenty-four hours I didn't know where to look.

We managed to open the door, having let down the window and scraped away the snow from the handle. Ten yards from the car, Gerald stopped suddenly.

"Hear that?"

Sure enough a deep rumble came from somewhere ahead of us. As it got louder, a mountain of snow moved steadily forward.

"A snow plough! Quick! Back to the car!"

From the bonnet, we waved and shouted like mad to try to get the driver's attention. It was probably operated by computer and would sweep both car and newly married couple ahead of it. It wasn't until it was almost abreast of us that it stopped and a red-hatted teenager jumped from the cab.

"'Ere all night, then?" He stuck his tongue through bright pink chewing gum to make a giant bubble. Unfortunately, it didn't stick to his nose.

"It's OK. We're married," Gerald attempted levity.

"'Ard luck, Gov. Nuffin worse than being stuck in the freezin' cold with the trouble 'n strife."

I gave him one of my most withering looks but he just stuck his tongue through the gum again and blew. I was within an inch of flattening it against his face when Gerald put his arm through mine.

"Civilisation far away?" Gerald asked the chewing machine.

"Twenty minutes down the road. Garage 'n all. Missus can sit in my cab till you get back, if she likes."

"Em, she rather likes fresh air, thank you just the same." Arm in arm, we walked on the snow cleared road. "Another friend for life, Pips," Gerald laughed and planted a kiss on my cheek.

I refrained from mentioning qualities like "discerning" and "discriminating". Gerald can be naive at times.

It was none too soon when the gates of Woodleigh loomed before us, I felt more human, and realised, for the first time, it was home.

Letty and Flora were on the front steps to greet us.

"Thought you was never coming. Had you all dead and buried in a snowdrift."

"Only temporarily. The Sherpa's disciple came to the rescue."

Flora did a twirl in a new dress – blue with sprays of red cherries vibrating everywhere.

"Bought us some clothes, I did, with the money we made at the sale. Made two hundred and fifty pounds, all in, less what I owe you for cooking costs, of course," Letty said breathlessly. She looked almost beautiful in the Monday morning air, cheerful in a way she had never been before.

"There's no need to pay any cooking costs – the Aga was on anyway."

Seeing someone in good spirits was worth anything.

"And Flora can say your name."

Tiny curls bobbed as we all looked at her. Flora pointed a tiny finger at me and said: "PP, PP, PP," as she whirred about like a clockwork toy.

Letty blushed slightly.

"Don't worry Letty. I've been called worse things in my time," I reassured her.

"She's being potty trained. Probably found the two words the same."

Strange how adults feel let down by their children, as if what they say somehow reflects on them. Perhaps it does.

We helped ourselves to large Irish coffees and some vanilla slices Letty had baked from my recipe book, with a "Hope you didn't mind."

For the first time since she moved in, Flora seemed happy.

"Would you like to see what's in PP's bag?" I asked her.

She skipped over immediately to rummage in my tapestry holdall. In seconds she had the wrapping off. A yellow parrot with a fixed stare perched on a stick. Forever. I knew the feeling.

Flora's face lit up. A pair of tiny, fat arms gripped my neck. I lifted her onto my knee. The room was silent. She bent her tiny rosebud mouth and kissed me.

"Flora," I said, "that is the nicest thing that's happened to me in weeks."

We rocked and hugged for an age. For once I didn't care who saw my tears.

Letty shifted about the room. Gerald got up and left.

❦ *Chapter Eight* ❧

Stoat dropped in a Christmas tree "For the little'un" and Gerald kindly supplied the Ransome's collection of decorations, dozens of them, all in their original cardboard boxes. Flora and I set the tree in a bucket of water, and held it straight with some large stones.

"Flora making you slightly broody by any chance?" Gerald put his head around the door of the sitting room as Flora and I were busy decorating the tree.

"It's nice to have a child to celebrate Christmas with, don't you think?"

I turned to give Flora the silver wagtail.

"Here's the little bird, Flora. He likes to sit in the tree and watch the world go by."

"Bye, bye," she replied.

"How's the re-writing going?" I asked Gerald, in case he thought I was ignoring him.

"It's not. It's impossible to re-write something. It becomes a completely different book."

I felt like rushing in to offer advice, help, anything to help ease that look that spoke of loneliness and despair. But it would do no good. My solutions would not be his.

I handed Flora another silver wagtail.

"Seems to me you've been spending a lot of time with Flora recently."

I detected a distinct note of disapproval.

"Really?" I asked a retreating back.

The wagtails wagged drunkenly in the draught from the slammed door.

Married blisters.

It was true Flora was the focus of my attention. We connected. She accepted me totally in the way children do. No judgments.

Gerald was expecting the usual family Christmas – except this year he would have me at his side. The Sheepshanks, Mère, Père and Fille were to be there to make sure Pimmsy took his vitamin pills at this "trying time of year" and to encourage Mortimer in his psychopathic propensities. I felt like bringing my cavalry – Andy, Aggie and anyone else who cared to spend the festering season in shivering decrepitude.

However, Andy sent a card, saying he would be "busy". His "spiritual adviser" would be calling to see him. I didn't dare enquire further. Aggie and Eddie were "off to the sun" on account of Aggie's difficult year opening all those gin bottles. Eddie thought she could do with the vitamin D. Strange how relatives disappear like snow off a ditch when you need them most. Something about auras signalling distress makes everyone run for cover. I would just have to make do with Gerald locked in his misery, and Letty in her wish to be "anywhere but England" and preferably Kuwait.

However, there was still Flora. Within ten minutes every shiny ball and wagging bird was off the tree again, neatly arranged around the fender.

"Don't you want the Christmas tree to be decorated, Flora?" I enquired.

"Nice tree," she said.

She preferred things unadorned, simple. Her sense of tidiness got the better of her.

"Just be careful you don't put them in the way of Grandpa Ransome's unsteady feet," I demonstrated Pimmsy's unique, swaying gait. Not stupid was our Flora. She understood immediately and began to giggle and did her own impersonation of twirling a moustache and tripping over the furniture. I felt it was naughty of me to encourage her but she didn't have the gift of the gab yet, so I indulged myself. By the end of the morning we had impersonated the lot of them, collapsing in a heap on the blue couch.

"Oh, Flora, you're the nicest thing in this house." Her little face looked seriously into mine. "You're the only thing with life and laughter."

She put those tiny arms of hers around me as if she understood.

"Flora, I love you," I said and began to tell her stories of "the old country", of fairies and goblins, of my animals at home and the ones who had died, especially Nanny.

"Nanny. Tree," Flora pointed to the Christmas tree.

Goodness knows what sorts of connections she was making, so I put a rein on myself and brought her to the kitchen for lunch.

That afternoon I paid my second visit to Gerald's mother's room to clear it out for the influx of sweaty bodies at Christmas. However, this time I brought an old bayonet in case the snake sculpture that had frightened the wits out of me last time tried anything fancy. Needless to say, I also took the precaution of fortifying myself with an Irish coffee.

In fact, in the light of day, the snake looked almost friendly. Its body was transparent. Inside were dozens of tiny boats, each carrying a foetus. The myth of the fecund snake, populating the world, a fertility symbol with the Turcana. I ran my fingers along its head, down its back and curled them round its tail. I think I prayed.

"What on earth, Philippa!"

Gerald.

I tried to hide the bayonet. Unsuccessfully.

"What is going on?"

"Nothing."

"That is patently not true. You are in here. You are carrying a bayonet. You were massaging a snake. There is something going on. Something very strange."

Gerald should have been a barrister. I felt like the accused in the dock.

"You gave me the fright of my life coming in like that!"

Attack is always the best form of defence.

"Ever since we came back from London – in fact ever since you looked at Mrs Arnolfini, you've been in rotten form."

"It sounds as if you've answered your own question."

"No need to be so flippant, Philippa. I want to know what's going on."

"I happened to come in here and look at a snake and you find some fault with that! Most of the time you couldn't care less what I'm doing you're so glued to that bloody computer of yours."

"No need for the foul language."

Trust me to let the side down. Betrayed by an Irish coffee. However, onward, ever onward.

"Let's not get side-tracked with another accusation," I said. "I *am* cross. I keep out of your way, get the house into some sort of order, clear the garden, plan a free range chicken business and I'm going to put up with your relations for Christmas — what more do you want?"

"I simply want to know what is on your mind. You've become inseparable from Flora, even Letty says you're like a second mother to her. You're in here armed to the teeth fiddling with a fertility symbol. I'm sure there must be some sort of explanation."

"Seeing you're so perspicacious and insightful, I'm sure you'll find one to suit you."

I aimed the bayonet for the centre of the bed but missed by several yards. It clattered unceremoniously to the floor.

Christmas was going to be fun.

The following morning, Letty, Flora and I cleaned the turkeys that Mr Stoat had 'acquired' from someone he knew, ready to bestow on the lucky half dozen members of *Woodleigh Enterprises* who were able to produce a bucket of worm compost.

"That can't be right!" Letty said, staring at Gladys's note that one person had managed to produce two buckets of compost. "That must be Mr Skatch, you know — that thin, little wiry fellow that was all against it to begin with."

"In that case, Letty, he's extremely poor and needs a turkey badly."

I wondered how many people were going to have a miserable Christmas, unable to buy presents for their children or the little extra luxuries that made the whole business something to be looked forward to.

"Perhaps, Letty, we could give people a cake – just a small one."

Poor Letty's face registered consternation.

"Of course, I will pay for them."

She relaxed.

"I'd be happy to make them, Philippa. I've got some decorations left over I could let you have cheap."

Thanks a lot, seeing I bought them in the first place.

The cakes were ready, marzipanned and iced by the time the entire cast of *Woodleigh Worms* arrived for a Christmas Eve glass of mulled wine and mincemeat tart.

Mr Manifold was all spruced up in a suit he must have had for his Confirmation. His face was scrubbed to a shine and his hair oiled down with what smelt distinctly like Cheno Unction. From inside, however, his heart shone like a beacon on a dark night.

"Good te see you, Mrs," he said, shaking my hand until it was numb. "Good te see you."

And he meant it.

"It's very nice to see you, Mr Manifold. I hope *Woodleigh Enterprises* is still going strong."

"We miss you, a'course. Not a very, what you

might say – though it's a very unchristian thing to even think – *nice* man, Mr Hazlett. Not cheery. But then, not everyone is like your own good self."

"No need to single me out. There are lots more who are interested in helping."

His blue eyes screamed with hurt. Trust me to toss back a wonderful compliment from a simple, sincere man.

He put a hand inside his jacket and brought out a crushed, brown paper bag.

"A nice perfume, I alus think."

Miraculously, the bunch of sweet pea were still intact and smelled heavenly.

"Thank you, Mr Manifold. I'm . . . touched."

His blue eyes looked pleased.

"How did you manage to grow these at this time of year?"

"Them new artificial lights and plenty of liquid seaweed."

If only babies were as simple.

Letty came along with the mulled wine. The sensible woman had filled tankards with the brew. No polite thimblefuls for these hard-working folk.

Gladys and Canon Goodhew seemed to be having an argument about a mince pie. Goody-goody two shoes went to see if she could help.

"Very nice to see you both," I smiled my usual. "Are you about to sample one of my famous mince pies or deciding it's not worth the risk?"

Not a smile. Even the Canon's eyes looked slightly dead.

"Mrs Ransome," Gladys addressed me formally, after all that had been between us. "I was telling Simon that the mince pies almost certainly contain alcohol, at least a pint in all of these, if I'm not mistaken."

She was absolutely right but I kept my mouth shut.

"If Simon eats one, that's part of his Christmas ration docked."

"But it's food, Gladys; surely the same rules don't apply. For one thing, the alcohol has evaporated in the baking and for another its addition is merely preservative, not pleasurable."

A twinkle appeared in one of the Canon's eyes.

"I think if you care to sniff one, you'll agree there isn't a trace of mountain dew."

Both the Canon's eyes now twinkled.

"Just what I was trying to tell her."

"Try one yourself, Gladys," I suggested.

She gingerly bit into one. My mince pies are, of course, perfection.

Her eyes lit up. A dollop of rum was what the poor woman needed. I must introduce her to the joys of wine-tasting. Christ himself said to take a little wine for the stomach's sake.

Mr & Mrs Skatch sat beside the fire, glued to each other, obviously enjoying the mulled wine. I warned myself not to feel sorry for people but went to offer them some mince pies, just the same.

"Well, Mr Skatch, how did the composting go in the end?"

"Never had such a good time. Local pub gave us all their peelings and scrapings. Some of it got to worms' bellies but the chicken legs and stale sandwiches went into the Skatch's!"

Mrs Skatch looked at me as if I might be about to deliver a slap.

"That is good news. Waste food is such a dreadful thing. I suppose you'd need to be sure you wouldn't get poisoned."

"No fear a'tha'," said Mrs Skatch, swilling back the dregs of the mulled wine. "Pop it all in microwave."

I supposed they also had a television in every room and a video recorder. Perhaps these things made up for other deprivations, like food.

"Canon's talking about growing vegetables, digging up the old allotments."

"Good," I injected a modicum of enthusiasm. "Nothing like fresh vegetables."

"Not worth it. By the time you've finished buying the seeds and bug killer, there's not much difference."

I didn't argue about saving seed from year to year or gardening with nature in mind *à la organique*. The Skatchs had dragged me down to their level; nothing depresses like depression.

I made my way to the kitchen to fortify myself with a glass of vintage port and put the sweet peas into water. Always rainwater, never water from the tap. Look what drinking chlorine has done to the mass of humanity! No need to inflict it on flowers too.

"More," Flora held out her mug as I poured the port.

"Well, Flora, your little liver is about the size of one of these flowers, so it can't deal with alcohol very well. Tell you what, we'll put a dropperful into a glass of water."

The dropper held her spellbound. She took it in her tiny fingers and watched as the water magically shot up the glass tube.

"Don't put it in your mouth, Flora. Very dangerous."

"Dangerous" was a word I had been teaching her. Letty's attitude was to "live and let learn". I preferred to teach some caution.

"Philippa! Why on earth are you in here playing with that child when people need to be looked after?

Gerald in top form.

"Have some wine and a mince pie."

Perhaps that would do some cheering.

I put both into his hand. A few swallows and the lines above his brow eased.

"These mince pies are particularly good."

You don't realise what a prize you've got.

I re-filled the glass and heated some more pies.

"Sorry, Philippa. I'm in very poor form."

"All this re-writing, is it?"

"Partly. I haven't been able to tell you before now. I was too busy trying to cope with it myself. While we were away in London Mortimer seems to have done some mischief to my hard disc."

He put down his glass and looked straight at me.

"Of course, I hadn't taken a back-up. Weeks of work lost."

I sat down, pulling Flora close to me, clinging.

"I wish you wouldn't do that, Philippa, or – at least do it to me!"

I felt the cry from his heart. My arms were around him in seconds. He buried his head in my breast and with a heavy sigh, began to sob.

"Kying," Flora's little head poked under my arm.

"Yes, Flora. Gerald is sad."

A tiny hand rubbed his back.

He lifted his head.

"I see what you mean, Philippa. She's a really nice little girl. Just like you."

There wasn't a dry eye in the kitchen.

"There you are!"

Gladys.

"Oh, am I interrupting something?" she asked, drawing back.

I reached for some kitchen paper to mop up the

stray tears. Gerald always carries a proper handkerchief. I wonder how he manages to keep them clean. I've never seen them in the wash. Flora used her sleeve.

"No, you're interrupting nothing, Gladys. Nothing at all."

"It's just that . . . well . . ."

"Yes?" I encouraged. Not like Gladys to be so hesitant.

"We could do with some more mince pies."

Gerald gave me an admonishing look. That man was getting to know me too well. I would have to develop inscrutability. Soon there'll be no fun left in life.

"Of course, Gladys. Just what I was thinking. There's plenty more."

I took another two dozen from the Aga, shook some icing sugar over them and gave her the tray.

"You were right, as usual, Philippa. There isn't the slightest bit of harm in them. In fact, all that fruit does you a power of good. After all, it's God's sun that dries it."

And ripens the sugar in the cane to make the rum – but I kept that to myself. Masterly self-restraint. Gladys padded off to bestow the riches on everyone.

Gerald had Flora sitting on his knee playing ipsy-wipsy-spider.

I felt *de trop* and went to see how the rest of the world was getting on.

A familiar shape came towards me in the hallway.

"Thought you'd gone to your bed!" Canon Goodhew said crossly.

"Without saying goodnight to *you*? Never!"

"Oh, Philippa, it's good to hear you say that."

His face grew alarmingly soft and took on a half-joyous, half-ingratiating look. He came closer to me than I felt comfortable with. The smell of garlic hit me like a hammer. Come back *Old Spice*, all is forgiven.

"Why do you start and seem to fear me? to paraphrase the Bard," he came even closer.

"One of the things I hated about Spanish churches was the reek of the old *allium sativum*."

"But it's known to keep vampires at bay! It's what kept the builders of the Pyramids healthy. Ulysses would never have escaped from Circe without it!"

Circe was probably delighted to be rid of him.

"However, Philippa," he came alarmingly close, "if it's what they call a 'turn-off', I'll switch to peppermint."

How to tell him it wouldn't matter what aroma assailed me, the dish would still not be palatable?

"There you are, Simon! You're missing all the mince pies."

Gladys again. Saved by the bell.

"Just talking about the merits of garlic to Pippy, Glad."

Gladys gave one of her girlish giggles. Very unendearing but then I'm only a woman.

"Yes, you must try it. We put a clove in each nostril at bedtime."

No wonder there are no children.

As I entered the room, I noticed that, in my absence, Stoat had installed himself by the fire.

"Delighted you could come, Mr Stoat. Mince pie? A piece of cake? A glass of mulled?"

"An Irish Coffee."

A man who knows what he wants. I tore out to the kitchen and rummaged in the freezer for the cream.

"Gerald, could you break yourself away from Flora and hack some cream from that container for Mr Stoat?"

"Of course!"

He seemed almost happy. Children are gifts of joy. If only . . .

"Strange thing for Mr Stoat to ask for."

Gerald gave me a look. "Why?"

"Not your average request. Irish Coffee is usually drunk by women who don't like the taste of whisky but quite like its effect."

"Well, perhaps Stoat isn't your average man."

"I keep meaning to ask you his christian name."

"André"

"André? Is he French?"

"No, not exactly. Here's your cream."

On my return to the festivities, Stoat was busily leafing through one of the books from the bookcase. I handed him his Irish coffee.

"You enjoy reading?"

"You can never have enough books, can you?"

"I like ones that are about things, that say something new," I confessed. "And you, Mr Stoat?"

"The history of the last war is what I read about nowadays."

"Isn't that all a long time ago?"

"For some p'raps. For others it never finishes."

"Old war wounds?"

"You could say that."

I didn't feel up to any revelations about horrific experiences, exterminated families or dead friends.

"It's always too easy to say the future will be better."

"Couldn't agree with you more, Mrs Gerald. To put it in a nutshell."

Stoat spoke with the earnestness of one who had seen everything. He downed the Irish coffee in seconds.

"Another?"

"If you would be so kind."

I trotted off to get some more frozen cream hacked and put the remainder of the mince pies into the oven. In the dim corridor that familiar shape emerged from the woodwork again.

"Pips," the Canon whispered, opening the door into a small, unused room that hadn't seen a vacuum cleaner for decades. The only natural light was from a dome in the centre of the ceiling. Gerald called it the games room. The circular gambling table was now gone, the gold wallpaper peeling like mad. I kept a respectful distance at the doorway.

"Another mince pie, Simon? Just going to shove some more in the oven," I turned to go.

With a deft flick of his foot, the Canon had the door shut behind me. In seconds I was imprisoned between two arms. Perhaps I ought to reduce the alcohol in those mince pies. On second thoughts, I spied the pilgrim flask glinting behind the open jacket. He'd been nipping into the games room for a quick swig.

"What can I do for you, Simon?"

"Thought you'd never ask, Philly. Gladys doesn't understand about a man's needs; she's totally unspiritual."

I was trying to grasp the connection between what he seemed to mean with what he said he meant. While a wondrous experience, sexual intercourse is definitely to do with the corporeal.

"Have you explained to her about these spiritual needs?"

I was playing for time, aware of the plate in one hand and the glass with a vicious stem in the other.

He relaxed slightly, looked at me like an abandoned puppy.

"Of course. I'm forever explaining how I'd like to bathe in the warmth of her breasts, have her ride high on the . . ."

"I see what you mean," I nodded so energetically I dropped the plate and the glass together, making a dreadful noise and whizzing open the door to reassure everyone that everything was all right, that I'd just seen a mouse. I closed the door on the male rat behind it and hoped it hurt.

The joys of hostessing.

"You OK, Philippa?" Gerald was concerned at my pallor.

"Nothing a sip of that light Beaujolais wouldn't cure."

I despatched the glassful in seconds and Gerald poured another.

"This partying is taking it out of you. Let me put the last of the pies in the oven."

"And another Irish Coffee for Stoat."

"I hope nothing's wrong."

"What do you mean?"

I wasn't graced with a reply. I finished my wine more in anger than enjoyment and turned to find

Flora curled up on the seat of the chair, her tiny chin resting on her chest, fast asleep. I hoped when she got to my age she'd be just as sensible.

As I watched the light break through the camomile window the following morning, Gerald opened his eyes and stretched an arm towards me.

"Merry Christmas, Philippa," he smiled.

I felt lonely and tearful.

"My Pips not too happy this Christmas morn? Oh, Philippa, you're sad."

Two out of two for noticing. My salty tears seeped through the drawn threadwork on the pillow-case.

An arm snaked its way around me and pulled so that my back felt the prickles of a hairy chest. Divine. The goose could go to hell. I could always get Gladys to microwave it. But the pudding, my special pudding had to go on.

I jumped out of bed.

"Pips – you're not going?"

"No, I'm playing golf!"

A wonderful beginning. The day could only get worse.

I heard the tinkle of music as I passed the sitting-room. Flora, in front of the tree, Christmas paper everywhere. On her lap was my present to her.

"Sing song," she said, squirming with delight

and opening the musical box which held a miniature farm in cast bronze.

"Good present?"

"Woof, woof. Oink, oink," she said holding up the dog and pig.

"One day, Flora, you will come to visit my little farm and meet the piggies, the sheep and Poppy the cow."

She looked at me wondering and turned to the music box. I rewound it for her. It tinkled "Ba ba black sheep". Not politically correct at all. "Pigmentally challenged" is no doubt more acceptable though surely confusing; the two animals have nothing in common.

Flora now turned her attention to a cooking set, whisking imaginary egg whites. Copying her mother – so long as she chooses a more appropriate mate.

The phone rang.

"A very merry Christmas, sister."

Agatha, not sounding as if she'd just come from the cocktail cabinet.

"And the same to you. Spending it where?"

"Dingle, with Eddie."

"Thought you were going to soak up some vitamin D in the Canaries?"

"Someone called Clara wanted to come with us, so Eddie changed his mind."

Mo, Clara's boyfriend of last year's holiday, must

have outlived his usefulness. Clara was on the trail again.

"Dingle's hardly the cosiest spot for a mid-winter holiday," I suggested.

"Eddie says we can watch the waves."

Sounds wonderful.

"I've a bit of news, Philippa."

You've joined AA. You'll never touch another drop.

"You're going to be an auntie."

"Glorry and Andy?"

"Why, just for once, couldn't you think it was me who had something wonderful to relate?"

A big sister is always in the wrong, *ça va sans dire*.

"When is the happy event?"

I sounded hollow, even to my ears. The thought of a baby being born with the DT's made me shudder.

"And I haven't touched a drop of spirits since I got the news. I'm sticking to sherry."

The tipple of maiden aunts and clergypersons, not to mention the thousands who give up the gargle for Lent every year.

"And Eddie. It's his I presume?"

As soon as it was out I knew I'd said too much.

"Sometimes Philippa you're really hard to take. Yes, it's Eddie's. Not exactly intentional but we're very happy about it."

"So, does this mean you and Eddie are – more than good friends?"

"You never could just accept things, think the best. There's always the niggling."

I thought her remarks grossly unfair. She was probably suffering from an imbalance of hormones. By the twentieth week she should be as near normal as it's possible for her to be.

"Well, have a lovely time by the seaside. Watch out for the seventh wave."

The widow maker, the family wrecker.

Gerald appeared as I hung up.

"Everything OK?" he asked.

"Aggie's expecting a baby," I tossed at him and made my way to the kitchen.

Letty was there before me. The pudding was bubbling away, the goose already beginning to give off its oily aroma.

"Letty, you're a genius," I said.

"Veg is all ready to go whenever you like. Apple sauce for goosey gander is done and cooling."

"Good, I hate hot apple sauce, particularly with butter in it, as some people seem to think it should be."

Gerald stood at the kitchen door, staring.

"Can I have a word with you, Philippa?"

It didn't sound very inviting. Feeling cowardly, I declined.

"Perhaps later?"

"Definitely later."

By midday the Sheepshanks had arrived, threatening to smile but never quite managing it. They're probably hilarious at funerals.

I pressed a stiff drink into their hands.

"Bottoms up," I said in my jolly Christmas voice and re-filled the glasses. Perhaps if they were rendered comatose . . .

I watched Flora reach out to the youngest Sheepshank. A flicker of something animated young mutton's face but died almost as soon as it had begun.

"Letty, time to put the veggies into the steamer and take some of the juices from the goose."

"Here, let me do that Letty, it's too big a fellow to leave to a mere woman," Gerald gave her one of those winks I thought he reserved for me.

But I might have guessed. Showing off in front of his sister. She looked at me as if to say "the Ransomes are such wonderful people". One of these days . . .

"Seen Morty, Gerald?" she asked him.

"Rarely nowadays. Busy with his horse and a friend in the village."

"He's such a popular boy."

With about two people, himself and his sister. Three is a crowd, after all.

As if he had been eavesdropping at the door, Mortido entered the room.

"There you are Morty Torty!" Mutton Mère shrieked as the hairy bulk of misery sidled into the room. "Glad to see your friends could spare you for Christmas din-dins. Come and see what Sibby-Wibby brought for you."

One of the few occasions in my life when I searched for a puking bowl. Not to mention trying to contain the anger I felt at such misplaced sugary talk for one of the most spiteful people I'd ever had the misfortune to meet. Even Flora crept towards me and put her little hand into mine. I watched Gerald hesitate as he lifted the goose from the oven. He dealt with Mortido by ignoring him but that obviously took years of practice. My intestines did an internal summersault. I wanted to take the bread knife and do some criss-cross shapes on Mortido's head. Instead, I decided to quit the scene and, taking Flora's hand, I slipped quietly out the back door.

We walked down the little hill at the back of the house towards the lake, following a tiny stream no more than six inches wide that somehow managed to escape the depredations of the landscape re-designers. Across it were the remains of two old bridges made from wooden planks laid by Gerald in more innocent days. Flora tip-toed across one, only to discover that she was alone, that somehow I was left on the farther shore, at which she came running back in panic to grab my hand. An insecure child. Her absent father had a lot to answer for. I thought about Aggie and her expected baby and wondered what demon made people have children without an adequate home. Even birds with their tiny brains built nests.

"Juck, juck," Flora squeaked. Overhead three ducks flew in formation towards the centre of the lake, wheeled around the tiny island in its middle and flew over us again, honking for all they were worth. Though Christmas, the weather was mild. On my farm at home I was certain the pigs would have to put their tender snouts into cold earth, stiff with frost.

The lakeshore was reedy up to where the water lapped and then gave way to a narrow edge of sand. The rowing boat stood idle, like the one on Aran that Sven and I spent the day on, returning to harbour sans wine and virginity. Everything seemed less complex then, with only myself to look after.

"Well, Flora, I don't think we'll be missed for half an hour or so."

I pulled the cover from the boat, rolled it up and then lifted Flora.

"Now, Flora, put Teddy in the corner, where he can see everything, and you sit on the seat. As you can see, it's nicely upholstered to ease the delicate bottoms of the duck hunters. That's where they carry their brains."

I clambered aboard, causing us to wobble, much to Flora's delight.

"Wobble, wobble, wobble," she said, clapping her hands as I put the oars into the rowlocks, untied the rope and set off for the tiny island.

We sang *Row, row, row the boat* and *Speed bonny boat* – or at least I did and Flora made some unintelligible noises in between words like "boat" and "king". The wind tossed her tiny curls like thistledown about her face and rubbed her cheeks to a soft pink. How I wished she were mine, part of me. And yet she was, sitting there laughing and singing, showing me her joy and pleasure.

I brought us to where Gerald had shown me was the easiest place to land. That particular day, when we had brought our picnic basket and champagne to celebrate our first month together, seemed like an age ago. I looked around for reminders of it and found none. The trail had grown cold. Like our love? I shivered as I lifted Flora from her seat and set her down on the shingle.

"Kying," she said, looking into my eyes. No fool is our Flora.

"Yes, a bit sad, Flora. Nothing ever stays the same; life is constant change." Some changes to be borne in gratitude, others with fortitude.

"Enough of this misery, Flora. You and I are intrepid travellers, have just alighted from our galleon to land on enemy territory. Let's go exploring."

We crept our way towards the top end of the island, fingers on our lips making loud 'shushing' noises and ruining it all by laughing.

"Ah, here we are, a treasure chest I see before me. Follow me."

Marked with a stone slab was the sunken trough Gerald's mother had placed to house the necessities for an island picnic – camping Gaz burner, cigarette lighter, blackened kettle, a canister with tea leaves, a jar of milk powder and a tin of biscuits. The rule was that whoever witnessed the demise of any item was to replace it next time. So far the system seemed to work as the island was one of Mortido's pet aversions. I was glad somewhere was free from his evil presence.

We delved deeply into the trough and extricated everything, piece by piece. Flora was more taken than I would have wished with the gas burner. How to let her feel the heat without going home with burnt stumps for fingers was the dilemma.

"What on earth is that winking at me?" I asked Flora, who merely stared in reply. Lying on the grass was what looked distinctly like the incised pattern and chained stopper of Canon Simon's pilgrim flask.

"Knew you'd come, Pips. Just knew it. Don't look so startled! And you, Flora, don't cry, it's only Canny Simey."

I struck earth with a thud.

"That's it, Pips. Take it easy."

"Don't call me Pips!" I shrieked.

Strange how we say the stupidest things when we're absolutely flummoxed.

"It's Christmas Day!" I managed to say. "Isn't that the busiest day of the year for anyone with a dog collar?"

"Only till one. I slipped out while Glad was stuffing the chicken with chestnuts. I had this overwhelming feeling you'd be waiting for me. And – I was right!"

"I just happened to get into the boat on the spur of the moment! Nothing premeditated at all about it!"

"No such thing as 'just happened'. It's all of a piece."

Standing on the slight hill, he intoned like a Biblical patriarch, complete with outstretched arms.

"Ever since, Philippa . . . Ever since I cast my sinful eyes upon you, tasted nectar from your cocktail cabinet, watched you take command of a motley crew of mortals, witnessed the enthusiasm for things vermicular you engendered into the most cynical of men, stood by as Mr Manifold, that most retiring of countrymen, unfolded like the petals of a rose to reveal his heart of gold. Philippa, it's all due to you! You alone have rejuvenated a tired parish, awakened a palate jaded from welfare payments to savour the delights of 'doing it yourself'. In short, I love you."

The rest was a blur. The fluid in my ear canal made such a wave that it bashed against the drum and temporarily deafened me. The body is merciful. It protects us from pain. Somehow Flora had crept underneath my armpit and was now nestling in the shelter of my breasts, her thumb in her mouth.

"I get the feeling, Philippa – correct me if I'm wrong – that your feelings towards me are not as . . . engaged shall we say, as mine towards you. Be that as it may. I'm a patient man."

I felt something like a volcanic eruption beginning somewhere around my toes and climbing.

"Canon! I have never harboured any passionate feelings towards you at any time. I enjoyed your company. It seems that my goodwill towards you has given you the wrong impression!"

With some men mere politeness from a woman is taken as something glandular. Would that life were so simple.

"I think, Mrs Ransome, you are what is known in the trade as a tease. Marriage seems to give some women a licence to trifle with men's feelings, a 'you can't catch me' game. You have let me down badly."

"The only person who has let you down, Canon, is yourself."

The air was quite still for a few moments. Something had struck home. I hoped it wasn't just the whisky. I didn't dare lift my head in case I appeared triumphant. I felt his shadow come towards us and got myself ready to spring away but he stopped.

"Pips, what on earth should I do? I really feel I'm in love with you, but you're like the Virgin Mary, untouchable."

Thank God for that. The fates were smiling on me at last. Even Flora perked up a bit.

"Perhaps, Simon, you could begin with Gladys. She's . . . you know, she's aching just as much as you. Aching to be noticed. That's really what love is, in the end."

"Would she . . . have me, after my neglect of her?" His mouth tightened again. "She's pretty stuck in her ways. You don't really know her. She can be an awful woman."

"Then she's as human as the rest of us. Give it a try. No one's so stuck they won't respond. She may be a bit cross and hurt to begin with, but don't let that put you off."

He picked up his pilgrim's flask and turned towards the water.

"It's the trying that's important," I said to his back. Not a twitch. Minutes later I heard the splash of oars on water. At least he didn't try to walk on it.

I peeked at Flora's little face. Fast asleep. The only thing to do in the circumstances.

"Where on earth were you this time?" Gerald asked on our return, his face red from bending over a hot stove. "We've waited dinner – or, to be absolutely honest, I've deliberately delayed it until your return. Going off like that, without a word. Really, Philippa, this is the giddy limit." He bashed the potato masher on the side of the saucepan with greater force than really necessary. Perhaps this was the latest symbol of macho power.

Flora ran to Letty. I pulled out a chair and collapsed into it.

"Are you all right?" Gerald came towards me, concerned this time. "It's not like you not to fight back. What's the matter?"

I felt I was inside a tight drum. The world was going on outside, but it had nothing to do with me. I was a bent reed, not quite broken but fairly lifeless.

"Philippa, say something! Anything! Curse and swear even."

Still nothing. Nothing would come. I had no answers.

"Oh, be like that! Nothing like Christmas spirit to make you glad to be alive." He slammed the oven door shut, flung his apron across the room and went off to make love to his word processor.

Strange how people become cross when things aren't going their way, as if it was all my fault.

Playing patience was beginning to pall and my third hot whisky tasted less sweet than the other two. Letty had announced that the goose was well and truly cooked.

"If it's left any longer it'll need an urn," she moaned. I hated Letty's moans, always deep, heartfelt – the way I would probably feel if I gave in to my baser instincts.

So, the goose was carved. Flora persuaded Gerald to descend from his solitary lair and invited the rest of the clan to partake. They poured themselves into the room in various stages of inebriation. I was already seeing double, so I probably had a headstart.

"Sibby, do come and sit here," I slobbered at Mrs Mutton. However, while the old jungle juice renders me into affability itself, it seemed to do its worst to old Sib. She glowered at me in the way a ewe does if you dare to touch her lamb. Whatever vestiges remained in her once human body were torn to shreds by the demon drink.

"Now don't stand on ceremony," I cajoled, encouraging the motley crew to take a pew.

Pimmsy slithered along the wall, took a few precarious steps to grab onto the back of a chair and finally lowered himself into a heap, just where he shouldn't have of course. Mortido belched loudly which sent waves of hilarity through Sibby and Pimmsy, both looking at me to see how I was taking it. I pretended not to notice and tossed back the remainder of my aperitif.

Gerald arrived, silent and cross-looking.

"Whoever invented Christmas has a lot to answer for," I said by way of making conversation. "Of course it was unheard of until Dickens and then the retailers realised what a good thing they were on to. One razzmatazz ever since. So madly, madly gay."

Gerald gave me the most withering look ever; pure, unadulterated dislike.

I experienced one of those rare, painful moments of lucidity, when suddenly reality strikes you with the force of a kango hammer, much as a drowning person sees their entire life spread before them. What on earth was I doing here? Obviously a convenient receptacle for all the hatred and anger of the Ransomes, a scapegoat. I took in a deep breath.

"While we are all gathered here, on this auspicious day," I began, worrying that I would have some trouble with pronunciation. Not a bit of it. Emboldened, I continued: "I would just like to say, I have had enough of Woodleigh and all who sail in her, enough of the petty meanness and downright nastiness of the Ransomes, enough of trying to please everyone, enough of slaving away without appreciation. I have a perfectly good home and a most enjoyable life that I should never have left and which I shall go back to and hope I never have the misfortune to clap eyes on any of you again."

"Philippa, are you including me in all of this?" Gerald asked, astonishment written all over his handsome face. Even in *extremis* I noticed that.

"Yes," I said loudly. "You had the absolute cheek to be cross with me. ME whom you're supposed to *love*."

I strode from the room in a state of total upset for some unknown reason. They say you'll feel better if you say what's on your mind, get it off your chest. Total rubbish. You feel worse.

I went upstairs to fetch my coat and walking shoes. I heard Gerald's step behind me.

"Pips, you're not going. Like this! Today!"

"Today is as good a day as any. Once you discover something, there's no going back."

He grabbed my hand and held it for an age.

"I know what you mean, Pips. But your going won't change the reality, it will just make things more difficult for you. And it will make those appalling relations of mine feel they've won."

"I don't care any more whether they feel that or not," I said, feeling wooden, remote.

He put my hand to his lips and kissed it.

"Tell you what. If you can hang on for another day or two, both of us can go and stay at your farm."

Like the wave dragging the sand back towards the ocean, I felt my resolve crumble. An edge of something, however, kept me on the shore, a stone embedded in the sand, too deeply buried to be dislodged.

I put my hand on his head and smoothed his hair. Such soft hair.

"I really need to go, Gerald. For me. Not tomorrow or the day after. But now."

He kissed me gently on the cheek and took both my hands in his.

"Philippa. I love you. More than I love anything else and," with a slight laugh, "almost as much as I love myself. I admire you and I like you, everything about you from your challenging retorts to your fondness for a glass of good wine. There is no one like you. You're special. And brave and . . . good."

He squeezed my hands and then let them go.

My arms weighed a ton as I finally got them into my coat sleeves. My walking shoes took an age to lace up. Neither designed for the dramatic exit. The bending made me slightly dizzy.

"Listen Pips, you're too, em, tired to go just now. Why not have a snooze and go early in the morning, before the others are up."

The seventh wave came hurtling towards the shore, pulled the sand from around the stone, dislodging it. Holding fast sometimes takes too much of an effort. Gerald helped me undress, tucked me into bed and fetched me a large glass of water. Essential to avoid a hangover.

"Sleep tight," he whispered and left to join the family fray.

❧ *Chapter Nine* ❧

It was well into the morning by the time I had surfaced. Gerald's pillow was ice cold. I donned my plumes and sneaked down the stairs. Not a sound. Though almost noon, no one was up to witness my departure. I walked through the mist, down the driveway and towards the Rectory. The only thing I brought with me was my credit card. I would send for my bed linen later. Sheets are torment on a jumbo jet.

The rectory door opened a crack.

"Oh, it's *you*."

I didn't feel strong enough to enquire whether the 'you' was good or bad.

"I need a lift to the airport, Gladys. Any chance you could oblige me, say within the next five minutes?"

The door opened another inch.

"That's at least a two hour drive, Phillipa! Some tragedy? Dead animal?"

d said, "I have to get

veal Gladys in her
l more than was
rm breasts were
tretch mark in
plain face but

e doesn't expect visitors on
pulled at a stray curl on her neck
dreamy look in her eye.
Simey, the Canon that is, came home yesterday
in a most . . . loving mood . . ."

She smiled, remembering. I wanted to say "lust
more likely" but restrained myself, though mad
with envy.

"Sorry he's . . . not available, Philippa. He's
extremely tired, so many services yesterday."

Not to mention last night.

She almost pushed me towards the sitting-room
with the picture of the dying child.

"Honestly, Phillipa. It's all so wonderful. I think
maybe it was you who reminded him what it was
like to be young again. Though," she leant towards
me giggling like a silly schoolgirl, "I almost
frightened him to death – 'Like wrestling with a
lump of barbed wire!' he said. I was just coming
down for the comfrey ointment and bandaid when I
heard the doorbell."

The mind boggled. The vision of mating they conjured up defied even my fertile imagination. Whoever said love-making was all soft lights and whispers? Mostly it's scratching, biting and bruising – if you're lucky. At least it takes one's mind off the weather and the price of petrol.

Gladys was dressed in minutes. The Canon had the grace not to appear.

"Isn't this a trifle sudden, taking off like this?" Gladys asked, placing a cushion on the seat and carefully lowering herself onto it.

"Nothing like striking when the iron is hot," I replied with mock gung-ho. "The only decent food a body can get is in Ireland."

"The Canon was just saying we must go over for a visit."

I remembered to forget to give my address.

The flight was full, complete with a bedraggled Father Christmas, a drunken sixty-year old with a filthy beard. He insisted on giving a "festive kiss" to everyone, men included. I pretended to be asleep, though I smelt his whiskery breath investigating me.

I got a taxi straight to Nellie's flat. Nellie was the only maternal figure in my emotionally deprived life, my rock in perilous seas.

"Philippa! What's wrong?"

Nellie noticed my swollen eyelids immediately.

"Everything, Nellie. Life has kicked me in the teeth. It was an act of absolute folly to think that pure, unselfish love exists, that marriage is a reasonable transaction. No one ever said you take on the family, lock, stock and barrel."

"Oh, dear," Nellie said. "When you start using clichés like that, things must be bad. Sit down and I'll make a cup of tea."

I curled up on Nellie's couch and fell fast asleep. I dreamt of water and babies and flowers and then of storm clouds and lightning and rolls and rolls of barbed wire. Even asleep we're in torment.

I awoke to find Nellie making another pot of tea and taking something delicious from the oven. I hoped they were jam tarts. Nothing like goo when you're feeling poorly.

"Afraid it's not jam tarts. Cherry pie. You used to like it – when you had more sense."

"Ignorance is not the same as stupidity, Nellie. I really thought everything would be all right. I really liked him and I thought that was all there was to it."

"If only . . . sure I'd have been married dozens of times if that were the case. Mostly they had a mother in tow, usually with a bad leg or back – though often as not just bad, full stop. Or maybe a father in the wings, just waiting till you were installed in the kitchen before they pounced at you with their 'special diets' and dirty underwear."

She poured the tea from the glazed earthenware teapot she cherished and handed me a chunk of cherry pie.

"Beats me why any self-respecting girl would let herself in for skivvying – or the other thing, for that matter."

That was the crux of the matter. Nellie was born with numbed nerve-endings just where it mattered to most of us.

"Only reason to get married, young Pippin, is for children. All of it would almost be worth it to have a little baby."

It was then I felt the ache I hadn't allowed myself to feel all these weeks. An ache to give birth, to create new life, to have a baby to hold; to look after.

"Now don't be getting upset. He seems a good man. It'll maybe turn out OK. Just hope for the best."

I threw my soggy tissue into the fire and put the cup down.

"Nellie, what was my mother really like?"

She started as if stung.

"I was frightened you'd ask me that one day. Not that I was keeping anything in particular from you. But still, it's better to think well of the dead, even if . . ."

"They were not particularly nice."

"You could say that. A spoilt woman, your mother was. Your father was run ragged with her, giving in to all her whims, trying to please her. But nothing did. Her heart was closed. Hadn't even time for any of her children. Signs on you all. You seem to have come out of it better able for life than the others, though. Clever, that's why. I used to watch you come into the house. A look was enough for you to see the lay of the land. Andy or Aggie never knew which way was up. They sort of cut themselves off. But you looked after yourself, kept clear of her."

"Maybe I won't be a fit mother then, even if I have a baby. Perhaps, as you say, it's all for the best."

"Now, no more of those tears. It will all work itself out. Because you *know*, you'll make a good mother. It's the people who don't bother to think about what they're doing that make a mess of it."

I helped myself to more tea and cherry pie. Food is such a comfort at trying times. A glass of wine wouldn't go amiss but Nellie's tipple is sherry. She swore she could "taste the grape skins" in wine.

"I forgot to wish you a happy Christmas, Nellie."

"I wasn't bothered. You never hear tell of Christmas in Jane Austen's time. I'll settle for that. Midnight Mass though, that's a bit of a treat with the church all lit up, the candles on the altar shining through the Arum Lilies and the pitch black outside. But you can keep your turkey and pudding."

I thought of the goose that I hadn't tasted, of Flora, who I hadn't kissed goodbye and the look of dismay on Letty's face. And Gerald, abandoned. Nothing takes the pleasure out of misery quicker than regret.

"You can stay the night, if you want. We could go to Stephen's Green in the morning and have tea in the Shelbourne."

Nellie's idea of heaven. All dressed up in her fifty-year-old camel-hair coat, sitting on an over-stuffed couch, drinking tea from a china cup.

"Definitely another time, Nellie. I just feel I want to get back to base, to my own four walls and piece of earth. Andy's coming to collect me; I phoned him from the airport."

Thankfully, Andy hadn't brought his dilsy with him.

"Glorrie sends apols – she's laid up with a bit of a headache. Said she'd throw something together for a bite to eat for us."

A headache meant only one thing.

"Andy, I hope my carefully laid down home brew is still maturing on the rack and not down anyone's gullet!"

"Now relax, Sis."

The appeal to our relationship roused my suspicions.

"Well, are the elderberry and rhubarb still safe, Andrew?"

His shoulders tightened slightly. A bad sign. Guilt. Perhaps I was better not knowing. It would be enough just to get home.

"Emily's been once or twice, nosing about everywhere," he said, sniffing. Another bad sign. "You ought to discourage her. She's very rude to Glorrie."

Good old Emily; obviously on my side. I felt very affectionate towards her. She cared.

"Why pick Boxing Day to come back? It's a holiday. We didn't have time to do a bit of tidying up."

"Look, Andy. It's my house, my farm. I can come back whenever I wish. You've obviously been caught on the hop. Well, too bad!"

The rest of the journey was blissful silence, empty Christmas roads, an air of sadness everywhere, dripping like the dew from bare branches.

Home was nothing like the image I had carried in my head of warmth, peace, rest. Emily hadn't exaggerated the clutter. The house was like a tip and smelt worse. Gloria stood by the cooker chewing her hair-ends.

"Look, Sis, just take a big breath. The chickens I can explain, and the dead cow. There's a perfectly good reason why the lamb got sick – and the new enterprise is going to change all our fortunes."

I wanted to scream. But settled for a yell.

"Just go you two! Go and find a room for the night. We'll leave explanations for the morning."

They look relieved and I half regretted not exploding, once and for all. But . . . would it make me feel any better or do any good?

I trod through the discarded clothes, half-eaten sandwiches and empty beer cans, and went upstairs. At least my bedroom was safe. I alone had the key. I didn't want anyone else relieving their urges in my sanctuary. It lowers the coinage of the whole business. Some things should remain sacred, like mattresses.

Well-known for its hard frosts and biting winds, the midlands can also play host to centres of high pressure that last for days. I woke up to one of these, with sun streaming into my room, though no camomile window. And an empty bed. I decided to deal with that feeling later, when I'd sorted out Andy's list of catastrophes.

The phone brought me downstairs.

"Pips – hello. You might at least have said goodbye."

Gerald.

A lump the size of a decent truffle sat on my vocal cords and refused to budge.

"Pips – are you not speaking?"

The urgency brought a squeak from me.

"Of course. Just a bit tired that's all."

"Not sleep well?"

"Like a log – it's just . . ."

"What do you mean 'like a log'? Wonderful to hear you have a decent night's sleep the first time you're away from your husband!"

"But I was tired. Why wouldn't I have slept?"

"You could have had the grace to toss and turn for even ten minutes. Nice to know you missed me terribly."

Trust me! Being able to lie is a virtue sometimes.

"I did notice the empty bed this morning though." Nothing but the truth.

"That was nice of you. Well, you obviously have very important things to do. I won't keep you."

"Gerald . . . ?"

How can you explain that a dead cow, chickens, sick lambs had taken over your thought processes? Perhaps Poppy was gone, her unborn calf never to see the light of day.

Nothing's fair in love and war.

The chickens I discovered whizzing around a circle of cardboard in the pantry. The health inspector would not be pleased. A layer of dust covered everything. They would have to go. Though it was hard to be cross with them, their fluffy bodies billowing on the top of needle legs barely visible as they scurried to the water fountain or pecked at the floor with tiny beaks. I decided to leave them for now. Nothing like the sight of helplessness to get the better of you.

As soon as I opened the back door, the odour of death hit me. Poppy, even dead, would never smell so badly. A dark shape lay slumped in a corner. Holding my nose, I went to investigate. Definitely not a Pippy Farm type. From somewhere beneath it, black slime oozed its way down the yard. The smell of rotting flesh defies description. It's one of those odours that grabs your entire body, saturates every pore, paralysing you for breath. I put a towel over my face and went to investigate. No horns. No udder. Definitely not Poppy. One of Andy's great money-making schemes. Probably got it cheap at the mart because it was ill. I ran to the phone and called the hunt.

"She's after being dead how many days?" a voice that sounded sixteen asked.

"Just in the last 24 hours," I lied.

"Is there a strong smell?"

"Just the usual."

"Afraid we only come if the animal is still warm. The dogs have a great taste for the maggoty meat but it's murder cutting it up."

Quite. He had my sympathies. I politely said goodbye and phoned the knacker.

"We've had that many calls we'd need a lorry and we only have a trailer. And the yard here is getting full 'cos it's the holiday season. The renderers don't open for a day or two."

I tried bribery.

"Well, we always charge £10 anyway, but £20 would see the job done."

I made a note to stop it from Andy's beer fund.

I stayed inside, gathering dirty clothes and trying to make the floor pattern come alive. The washing machine still worked: obviously not in tremendous demand. Gloria clearly came from the school of personal hygiene which felt *the clartier the cosier*. The loo was a different matter. Choked with paper and slow to flush. Perhaps the odd dead chicken had been despatched to the septic tank. I went out the front door to avoid the knacker's goods and made my way to the septic tank at the side of the house. The manhole displayed a blockage at the entrance to the tank from the sewer pipe. That was a job I was leaving to someone who enjoyed guddling in manure. Andy.

The store cupboard had been raided. Not a jar of beetroot, pickled onions, tomatoes, or chutney was left. As if an army of starving soldier ants had marched through on one of their extended campaigns. Even the empty jars were gone. However, I extracted, from beneath a secret panel at the back of the top shelf, a mixed tin of delicious sweetmeats. The sellotape seal had not been tampered with. I put the kettle on, cleaned the stains from a china cup and settled down to cheer myself up with a cup of tea. As soon as I opened the tin a cloud of spores, delighted to be liberated from their confinement, shot out. Their parents, in various shades of blue and green, remained glued to my caramel squares and vanilla fingers. Even fungi have to live, I suppose. I just wished, right then, that they had spared me a little treat.

The knacker person arrived, put his hand out for the money first and then got to work. His ingenious little winch arrangement raised the mound of flesh and gradually lowered it into the trailer to lie beside a dead dog.

"You do dogs too?" I asked, more in horror than curiosity.

"Anything dead."

"Well, I better not stand around too long!"

He gave me a stony look. I obviously wasn't worth the wait.

"Death's a serious business," he said as he got into the car.

"Expensive too," I said. However, like undertakers, knackers have no sense of humour. By the time the trailer had rattled its way out of the laneway, a gallon of Jeyes' fluid had made inroads into the black slime that remained. Nothing like dead animals to encourage you to take up vegetable production.

More acceptable aromas were wending their way round the kitchen from the batch of jam tarts and vanilla slices cooling on a rack. As if in reply, Emily poked her head round the kitchen door.

"So, it's true. I couldn't believe it! Philippa! Without Gerald! Never in all my life with Dickie – and there have been trying times I can assure you – would I have dreamt of going off without him. But then you're several years younger than me."

I waited till Emily needed to catch her breath to ask her if she'd like a mug of coffee.

"Thought you'd never ask. Just like old times. Go easy on the brandy."

I hadn't even thought of it, but a nod's as good as a wink. Except that the cocktail cabinet was empty.

"Sorry, Em, we're out of luck."

"Not to worry. I'll nip down to the village. Haven't had a decent chin-wag since you left."

A chin-wag was not on my agenda but "all is emptiness" as the Buddhists say, so I gave into it and sat staring into space until she returned. Woodleigh Hall popped into the void, a dismal, cold recollection, except for Gerald and Flora. They were the yin to the house's yang. I knew then I would never live there again, that I'd got out by the skin of my teeth. It's all very well to say *evil thrives where good people do nothing* but in real life evil has a motivation behind it, a purpose, which good rarely has, unless you're like Mother Teresa scraping dying bodies off the streets.

"I told her it was for cooking," Emily said defensively, on her return with half a bottle of brandy. 'But Christmas is over', said she. 'Sure doesn't the mincemeat dry out something terrible', says I. Nosy cow – though I shouldn't use those insulting words. This course I'm doing says just to 'be where you're at'. Hard at times when you've something gnawing inside you."

She poured a generous tot into the steaming coffee. I put a dollop of frozen cream to float on the top and watched it melt.

"We're also supposed to support our 'sisters', particularly against the enemy in trousers."

"There are certainly worse things than men, Em. Mind you, I can't think of anything in particular just now."

"So, the honeymoon is definitely over, Pips. It happens to us all, sooner or later. The smelly socks, the half eaten sandwiches strewn about the place. The thing I hate most is having to clean his shoes. To put my hand inside his shoes takes all the power of the Sacred Heart."

"You could always use gloves," I suggested.

She gave me a dirty look. We finished our coffee and poured another. Suddenly, a glow settled on the world.

"Do you know, Emily, there's no place like home."

"I wouldn't know. I've never known anything else. Went straight from my parent's house into Dickie's. But, come to think of it, there isn't a corner I could call my own, whereas he has the whole shootin' gallery. Who cares? We're supposed to give up all this longing for things of the world and lay up stores for the next. Still, all the same, wouldn't it be nice to have a space you could say was yours to put your bits and pieces on, make a mess of it if you want."

Emily was obviously getting maudlin.

"You're driving, Emily?"

She helped herself to another squirt of brandy and a dollop of cream, now recovered from its frozen state.

"There's plenty of time to sober up before I've to go and put the dinner on."

I resigned myself to a long day and put on Mozart's piano concertos.

"Has Andy got rid of that doxy yet? Never saw such a one. Always lying down."

I could well imagine.

"And everyone was talking about the strange goings-on. Lorries in the middle of the night, squawking sounds."

Hardly the chickens or the dead cow.

"Squawking sounds?" I asked, coming to slightly.

"Like a duck being strangulated."

"Emily, you're just what I need. How could I think there was no purpose to your visit! Put on the boots and I'll lend you a dungaree."

Suitably booted and spurred, we loaded the

range with fuel and put the kettle on top of it for our return. There was just enough brandy for a hot whisky.

"I think the best thing to do is go from one inch of the farm to the other, just to take note of anything peculiar."

Emily looked with some curiosity at the still visible black stain on the yard but tottered on, shrugging her shoulders. Her sight tends to go when she's had a few.

We made for the outhouses. In the first all seemed as it should be. Bags of rolled barley, shredded beet pulp and some bales of hay all neatly stacked, though somewhat diminished; not unusual for the time of year. In the second stall stood Poppy and her current calf.

"Well, Em, all is in order here."

"What's that smell?"

I didn't like to mention dead cows.

"What's it like?" After all, she could be talking about drinking chocolate or mouse droppings.

"Sort of rotten egg smell with an acid overtone."

"Emily! You've been watching too many food programmes on television."

"Serio, Philippa. Totally rotten egg."

We were in front of the largest of the outhouses. The original cart shed with arched doorway. Sure enough, in the channels sloping from it towards the yard drains oozed a brown liquid created by no animal or vegetable I was familiar with.

"God, what a stink!" Emily said, pulling back.

"See anything?" I asked.

"No. Driven back by the stench."

Not a thousand dead chickens . . .

A thud against the door made us both jump. It was alive.

"Pips, you go in. You've had more brandy than me."

She was definitely joking. I'd been counting.

I peered through Emily's crack in the door. Feathers. Not turkeys! Andy had been lamenting how tasteless they were nowadays.

I unhooked the wooden bar and pushed in one side of the door.

"Holy Mother of Cow, are we seeing things?" Emily squeaked.

I grabbed her just as she was about to run.

"God, Pips, let's get out of here. He must have been feeding them turkeys hormones. Look at the size of them!"

Their long necks stretched towards us, beaks open, a look of startled arrogance in their eyes like an angry school teacher.

"Look at the feathers! You'd be a month of Sunday's plucking them fellas. Never seen the like anywhere. Must have got a strain of these new hybrids that grow in ten weeks."

The two giant birds lifted their plates of meat and with a side wobble came towards us.

"Out!" I shrieked, narrowly missing Emily with the wooden bar and only just in time to stop a beak from whatever it was bent on.

We were silent for a minute or two.

"You'll never eat those turkeys in one sitting," Emily said, concerned.

"Emily," I said with as much composure as I could master, "Not turkeys. Ostriches."

"Ostriches? Must have escaped from the zoo."

"If only. We could give them back. They're the latest craze across the water."

"Brandy never did agree with me," Emily said, hugging her middle.

I never knew Emily's hair could get into such disarray. Whatever held her long tresses on top of her head had now disintegrated. Always attractive, she looked almost beautiful, her face framed in curls.

"Time for more coffee," I suggested, slipping my arm through hers.

"Sans cognac, this time," Emily said, a little wistfully.

"You have whatever you need, Em. Don't let little things like wobbly legs and dishevelled looks worry you."

She gave me one of her stares but I ignored it. What's the point in being able to speak if you can't have a slight joke now and again?

I lit the fire in the sitting-room and passed a

footstool to Emily. Within minutes she was snoring. I took out the piece of embroidery I'd started months ago, before Woodleigh. All past tense now. And Gerald. It is *not* better to have loved and lost than never to have loved at all. It's infinitely worse.

I ripped through a rose that had gone somehow askew and replaced the pink centre with deep red. Like blood. Love is always red roses and bloody hearts; we grow anaemic with hope and longing.

I had barely half a dozen stitches done when I put it down and felt a luxurious wave of nothingness creep over me. Then everything went blank, except for a vague sense that something was creeping upon me.

I woke to find myself snug beneath a duvet. An unknown donor. I listened for footsteps but all I heard was Emily's deep breaths as if she were struggling for air. Poor Em. She didn't realise how ill a turn life had dealt her. But do any of us? We seem to put off painful realisations until we are able to deal with them.

There was a noise in the kitchen. I crept from the duvet and tiptoed towards the door. Through the missing knot-hole I saw my one and only least-favourite brother help himself to a vanilla slice.

"Don't let a little thing like brotherly love stand in the way of your empty stomach!"

"Sis – you gave me one helluva fright!"

Good. If it weren't for the thoughtful duvet I'd have called the police.

"Now, dearest brother, explain those primeval arm breakers in the shed. Do you realise they can peck your heart out quick as look at you?"

"Not those Ossies. They're a little goldmine. They live till they're eighty years old, lay an egg a day each that's worth two hundred smackeroos. That's roughly £40,000 a year. And they only cost £24,000 a piece. Now beat that with your *caramel squares* or *vanilla slices*, etcetera, etcetera."

"I can see you don't object to the "odd vanilla slice" just the same. Let me tell you about ostriches. They're expensive, dangerous, they need heat, they stink, it takes twenty-three dead ones to fill a wheelbarrow . . ."

"Now you just stop there! Who said anything about dead 'uns? Healthy as larks those two are. And it's not just the eggs that are valuable. Lady Di has a pair of ostrich leather trousers and hatters would do anything for the feathers."

No wonder they call them "mad".

"Listen, Andy. There is no way on earth ostriches are going to make your fortune. They're every bit as bad as deer farming, except they don't throw themselves against fences just because they like the sight of blood, though some people I met at Woodleigh wish they would."

A sober look came across his face. The boyish enthusiasm had vanished. I almost felt sorry for him, except that the brutes were on my farm.

He put the kettle on.

"So, you know a bit about ostrich farming. I might have known."

"Here." I handed him the brandy bottle.

"What a cock-up."

"Self-flagellation will not solve anything, Andy my dear. What to do is the question."

I poured myself a stiff drink. As it slowly wended its way to my toes, a light turned on in my head.

"Could you give them back to whoever sold them?" I asked hopefully.

No reaction. Obviously not possible.

"How about encouraging someone to 'take them over' merely on a trial basis, to check that they would be 'good' owners."

A dirty look.

"Well, some people would be taken in by that."

I finished the dregs in the bottom of the glass and poured another.

"So," I said, wishing I still smoked, "it's to be ostrich soup for the next ten years. Not to mention feathers coming out of our lugholes, just when the fashion is for plastic flowers. Of course, I've never had an ostrich egg – at £200 a time there must be some eating on them. We could always sell them to restaurants offering 'Giant Breakfasts, the 'biggest boiled egg in town' – imagine sitting down to that after a night on the tiles! I know – we could blow the insides out of them, make mayonnaise for *Philippa's Pantry* out of the egg, cut the shells in two, hinge them and make little miniature nests inside for – guess what – baby ostriches!"

"For Chrissake, Sis. Give over."

"I could go on, but I won't. I think you get my drift."

I took the brandy with me and went to bed.

The headache after swilling the dregs of a bottle of brandy have to be felt to be believed. Wine gives a dull throb and giant thirst but brandy seems to jigger the entire works. I crawled to the bathroom and turned on the shower. I drank half the water and washed with the rest.

"An egg nogg is a great 'cure'" my father always said. Since egg was the last thing I wanted to have anything to do with, I had more water. A "hair of the dog" was the rocky road to addiction, so I decided on a glass of wine for lunch.

Emily's chair was empty. But she'd left a note on the kitchen table.

The animals are all seen to and still alive. Left the "turkeys" to their own devices. Loo seems a bit choked. See you soon.

Andy had gone, leaving one Vanilla Slice. I ate it, shivered and decided to go back to bed. Nothing like bed when you're feeling low. Except that it's empty. You get used to someone, begin to rely on them like an extra arm. Is it better to keep the heart closed, retain one's independence? At least you know where you are.

I made a flask of coffee, a large sandwich, tucked the box of chocolates Emily had left under my armpit and took off to my bed. The radio had a heart-rending Christmas play about someone not getting any presents. Disappointment writ large. Just what I needed. The end was reasonable – she went out and bought to her heart's content, on her husband's credit card! Still, too much revenge there for my taste. Just because someone pokes a burnt stick in your eye, no need to stoop to their level.

I sipped the coffee and let the chocolate melt away, the way love does when the going gets tough. And again, I thought about Gerald. I fell asleep thinking about Gerald. Who says coffee keeps you awake?

A swollen river had burst its banks, and carried me along, fearless, weightless. Tree trunks that had become snagged in currents ignored me, allowed me to pass unhindered. All was blue and green except in my head everything was red. A voice said: "Philippa . . . where are you? Where . . . ?"

I lost my weightlessness and tried to swim but I

got heavier and heavier and felt I was sinking, green and blue closing over my head.

"It's OK," a voice said. A familiar voice.

"Gerald!" I shot up in bed, wide awake, spilling the chocolates.

"Take it easy. It's bad for you to jump up like that. Take your time."

His face was soft and his eyes spoke kindness. I lay back. Hoping he'd leap in beside me, wishing he would take a mad fit of passion and need and want to have his way with me there and then. But Gerald's urges arose out of love not from mad, animal lusts. Unfortunately.

"How did you know . . . ?" I said, wanting to ask how he divined my need for him, the void I couldn't fill.

"I had to come. I have some bad news."

Some circuit in my brain went into overdrive, wanting to *know* at once. My mouth wouldn't part to ask "what?"

He put his arm around my shoulder, held me, and looked into my eyes.

"Pippy," he said gently. "It's Flora. She's dead."

Not that! I wanted to scream.

"When?"

"Yesterday, about 12 o'clock we think."

"You think?"

"Yes. We don't know for certain. She wandered

off as far as we can make out, about half an hour before that. She wasn't dead for long before we found her."

"And she was . . . ?"

"Yes. She'd drowned. We tried but . . . Letty would still be trying . . . but it was no use . . ."

Gerald's shoulder shook slightly. I put my hand to his face.

"Oh, Pippy, we had to pull her off Flora's little limp body."

I fell back against the pillows and tried to breathe. Flora gone. Drowning . . .

"What was she doing near the water?" I asked.

Gerald sighed. He took off his coat, folded it across the end of the bed and came towards me. He knelt beside me and took my hand in his.

"She wandered off down the stream towards the lake. She tried to climb into the boat, must have put one foot onto it, it moved . . ."

"God, Gerald, don't say it was my fault!"

"Of course it wasn't your fault! You weren't even there."

But somehow, it was.

"Philippa, you musn't even think it had anything to do with you. It was the rest of us who were to blame. We should have watched her more carefully. Letty was busy trying to cook and I was upstairs. Father is still in the drunken stupor he began at Christmas. So, Flora wandered off."

He was kind and didn't say it. Flora missed me. It hadn't occurred to me before. And I'd betrayed her trust, her precious trust. I didn't stop to think how important I was to her. I killed her with my thoughtlessness.

"Is there an inquest?"

"Yes, in two days but it's just a formality. She's lying at the hospital now."

"I must go to her." I said it as if it were the most obvious thing in the world. I had to see for myself.

"You mean — you're coming back?" Gerald smiled for the first time.

"To see Flora, yes."

What I really wanted to do was bury my head in the pillows and only come out when someone put the world to rights. But that is something we have to do ourselves.

I cooked some griddle cakes while Gerald checked the flight times. The smell sickened me. Slices of rubber and as appetising. Nothing, not even food, seemed important. Not even the ostriches. What did it all matter? Death has the ultimate power; everything we do lacks that.

I made tea and poured the water into the sink instead of into the pot. My mind was full of a dead child in a coffin, a nothing where there was once a mass of energy. Death is a closed door.

"OK, Pips?"

I nodded a lie.

"Really?"

Sometimes I wish Gerald wasn't so persistent. A wave came from my stomach and ended in my throat in searing pain. Gerald put his arms around me.

"It was an accident. These things can happen. Children can't be kept in cotton wool. They have an urge to grow, explore. We can't chain them to the kitchen table."

I didn't see why not. It was safer.

With a long sigh came one tear and then another. I buried my head in Gerald's shoulder.

"Why? Gerald, oh, why?"

But there was no answer.

Gerald had no appetite either. I made a present of the griddle cakes to the ostriches who killed them with jabs of their beaks. Their voracious appetite seemed cruel, heartless as death itself.

I phoned Emily and asked her to look after things till I got back.

"The death of a child is the worst thing of all," she said simply. "The poor mother will be tortured forever with guilt."

Except that Flora wouldn't have known about the boat if it weren't for me.

"I'll be happy to look after the animals, except for the ostriches. They're not normal. They have their eye on me."

I knew what she meant. They have an intensity about them.

"Ignore them. I've asked Andy to get them out of here."

Though they too deserved a chance to live. They were alive after all. And Flora was dead.

We were at Woodleigh before I felt I'd left home. Letty must have been watching from the window. She was on the step to meet us. One look at her face and I knew she didn't blame me.

"Oh Philippa, our little Flora gone," she said. We stood hugging each other, leaning on each other. "It's so hard to believe it. I still expect her to come running through the door. Several times I thought I heard her outside singing. Her little song."

The one I had taught her, that we sang together on the boat. Only days ago. She'd still be alive if I hadn't left. That was the cross I would have to bear. If only . . . If only . . .

"Come inside. I'll make some coffee." Gerald led me into the house and I led Letty. A miserable threesome.

"I'd like to go to see her," I said.

"So would I," Letty replied, "just to make sure it isn't all a dream. Though it would be easier not to go. To pretend."

Except the world doesn't allow us to do that for

long. There are things to arrange, people to contact.

"What about Flora's father?" I asked.

"I told his mother. She said she'd try and let him know. She told me she'd lost a child herself, a six month old baby and still remembers as if it were yesterday."

Flora lay in a room with two other children.

"All dead," Letty said. "Can you believe it? Three children on one day."

All that sorrow touching so many lives. One was about Flora's age, a boy with a bandaged head. Tiny and so still. The other was about ten, with long blond hair spread around the pillow, a black bruise on her cheek. I stared at these, not wanting to see Flora, avoiding the inevitable. But a low, deep groan from Letty made me turn to the bed in the corner.

"My little baby, my baby, my baby," she wailed, resting her head close to Flora's.

I went closer, dread slowing every step. And then Flora was before me, the Flora I loved, dead, forever. Never again that little voice whispering nonsense, those tiny fingers lifting decorations from the Christmas tree, those little legs running to meet me.

I lifted her hand and held it to my wet cheek and remembered her smile on the boat out to the island, her laughter as we sang and her fear of Canon Simon's ranting. She had lived totally. And died because she wanted to live a little more, pushing out from port to the world. But she didn't make it. She'd forgotten how little power she really had.

Letty's sobs held a world of mothers' sadness for a life which began with her and was now no more. There was no consolation for such a loss.

The following morning, Gerald and I carried Flora's tiny coffin to the dark hole in the village cemetery where she was to lie forever. Canon Simon spoke gently about Flora being free from mortal pain, while her soul travelled on its eternal journey. A robin perched on the mound of clay as if listening. Perhaps Flora was now a skylark or a silver swan like the Children of Lir. I wanted to believe there was something else, that the rattle of the gravel on the lid of the coffin did not express a finality. Choirs of angels and Heaven I had my doubts about.

Letty stayed behind when Simey had finished and the rest of us had said our goodbyes. She held a wreath of purple hellebore, their yellow anthers the colour of hope.

"She's all alone down there," Letty said.

I had noticed.

"I put Teddy in at the last minute," I replied.

"Not Teddy!" Letty wailed.

I'd done it again.

"I'm sorry Letty! It seemed so right, Flora adored him."

"But now I've nothing left. Not even Teddy."

How could I have been so stupid. Perhaps Gerald would retrieve him. Maybe the undertaker. In the midst of death . . .

I tossed in my tiny bunch of snowdrops and walked to where Gerald waited for me.

"Come and see this grave, Pippy," he beckoned. "There's a photograph of the grandparents, all slicked-back hair and dour looks. And see, there's a little baby with a wreath of flowers. Stillborn. And look at the one in the mother's arms 'Elsie: Lived for 10 days. Suffer little children to come unto me.' Seems strange that God should give and then take away so soon. Like a punishment."

"That's a little harsh. Death is everywhere, just as life is. It's *our* fears that make it into such an outrageous occurrence."

"All the same, it is harsh if a child is murdered or run over or accidentally drowns."

I couldn't argue with that. I resolved never to have children myself. I would soothe the ache of emptiness and longing as best I could.

"Gerald, before you dash off to another grave – Letty, she wants Teddy back."

"Is this a joke, Philippa?"

"No, afraid not. I put Teddy in Flora's arms before the lid was closed. Stupid me didn't think. It's the only tangible thing Letty had left. Flora adored Teddy."

"I see."

Two gravediggers hung on their shovels, waiting in the wings to bury Flora forever. Gerald and I looked at each other and, arm in arm, walked towards them.

"G'day Guv," the one with the damp roll-your-own cigarette said. His friend spat out the side of his mouth. Obviously the sort of position that attracts the least salubrious of characters.

"I suppose," Gerald said in his most diplomatic voice, "once the soil goes on, that's it?"

They stared back, at a loss for words.

"Unless, that is," Gerald put a hand into his inside pocket and took out his wallet, "it is delayed by weather, or something?"

"Somat like that, Guv," Damp Fag said. His friend spat with even greater energy.

Notes changed hands, a cigarette was stubbed out and the pair with the shovels crawled back into the woodwork.

"Just leave it to me, Pippy," Gerald said, hugging me.

I decided then and there to write to the Pope

recommending beatification for Gerald. Even if he was a Protestant.

Everyone had gone, except for Mr Manifold, who came towards me, hands outstretched.

"Ye know, Mrs Ransome," he said, glancing at Flora's grave, "it's like putting a little seed in the ground, it casts off its outer shell but its centre, its core, its . . . what ye might call, its essence, lives on."

I wanted to scream that Flora was dead, dead. She was gone, lost to us.

As if reading my thoughts on my face, he said in the sort of voice he would reserve for his sweet peas, "I know it's hard, lass. Ye'll not see her like again. Like a good bed of lettuce eaten by slugs or 'nihalated by frost, nowt you can do 'bout it. Just try again."

I looked at Letty, kneeling in the mud beside Flora, tears and snot streaming down her face, her hair wet from the snow flurries, her hands blue from cold. Alone, no husband to comfort her or promise her another baby.

"Letty?" I said.

She didn't register my presence.

"Come on, Letty, we must get you into a warm bath. Flora would want her mother to look after herself."

Letty looked at me puzzled. She was still locked

away somewhere like Hell with the furies around her, no comfort anywhere. Not even Teddy.

I lifted her from the sodden earth, and half carried her past the headstones of those who had died days, weeks and years ago.

"It's what'll happen to us all, 'suppose," she said.

Indeed. The one event we can be absolutely sure of. Just as long as we're not around when it happens.

Gerald had disappeared, leaving Letty and me and Mr Manifold to make our way.

"Can I drop you off somewhere, Mr Manifold, or would you like to come for some soup and a sandwich?"

His presence was strangely comforting, like a warm blanket.

"Never say no to a free meal," he smiled. "Free grub always tastes sweeter, like the slips you pinch from another's garden."

"Well, no need to pinch anything from Woodleigh. You are welcome to whatever you wish."

"Always liked you, Mrs Ransome. You've a generous heart."

Who would argue with that?

I doctored the soup up with pasta shapes, the sort Flora liked. She knew all their names. I added my salt tears to the pot.

Gladys appeared, with a glow to her cheeks. Looked like the Canon was still on his spiritual pilgrimage. She brought trays of sandwiches and a jam sponge – my pet aversion – but Mr Manifold's eyes lit up when he saw it. I decided that man really deserved a supply of caramel squares. None of the Ransomes made an appearance. Slurry, not blood, flowed in their veins.

"Didn't think we'd see you back so soon, on such a sad errand, Philippa. Makes me glad I've no children. I couldn't bear to lose them."

"We're caught whichever way, Gladys. Life without them isn't very exciting and yet having them seems to be such anguish."

"Well, Philippa, I've been thinking and what I've decided is to adopt a ready made one, maybe an orphan or a child with some sort of problem, so that if anything happened I could always say to myself: well, I did what I could and they got better than they were born to."

One way of escaping the responsibility of actually conceiving. I passed around the sandwiches.

Letty had disappeared. Alarm bells rang in my head. I handed Mr Manifold the jam sponge and told him to help himself and ran in search of her. The light in her room was on. I opened the door. She was sitting in the rocking chair, her arms folded over Flora's Teddy, staring into the blazing fire. I closed the door again and stepped back onto something.

"Gerald! You gave me the fright of my life. Just checking on Letty. She's got Teddy. She looks much calmer. Maybe she'll be all right. I'm thinking of taking her home with me."

"Home?" he asked.

"Yes. I'm going back in a few days."

"Oh, I see. I was sort of hoping . . ."

"Gerald, I really want to be with *you* but the constant presence of your family make even that pleasure sour as a sloe."

"I'm really sorry about them, Philippa. Somehow I must have felt that because I was inured to them, you would be too. But you're too sensitive for that, full of the milk of human kindness."

Two compliments in one day was really something. Could I get him to put it in writing so that the next time he disagreed with me, I could point to it . . . ?

"Nothing to stop you coming over to me, Gerald. We could share our lives on our own, without all this aggravation."

He looked thoughtful but didn't answer.

"By the way, how *did* Teddy get out of . . ."

"Stoat."

"Oh. Stoat?"

"And me."

That was all the information I was getting.

"And, was anything left in his place?"

"Yes. Dolly. She's more sensible. She'll look after Flora properly. Teddy's a bit of a flibbertigibbet."

Definitely sainthood. And soon.

❦ Chapter Ten ❧

Letty and I said goodbye to Gerald and Woodleigh on a wet, blustery morning, several days later. We went to visit Flora before we set off, the open grave now filled, a rain-splattered carpet of flowers on top.

"Why, oh why didn't I watch her?" said Letty. "She'd just disappeared for a minute. I remember I had finished putting the vegetables in the soup – I can still see every carrot and leek."

"Children have no conception of danger, Letty. Flora just decided to take some risks. You are not responsible for that."

"Even so, she might still be alive now, if . . ."

Altogether it was a sad, sad journey home.

At least the ostriches had gone, or been transmuted into something even worse. No dead animals, dirty clothes or mouldy food. The squatters had obviously not returned. Good old Emily. I phoned her immediately.

"You must be feeling awful, Philippa. The last time I buried a child it was Mrs Rowan's ten month old baby. A lovely, big boy. She wouldn't let them put the coffin in the grave, said the child would smother. In the end, the poor woman went mad altogether. They said the whole thing caused a blockage in her brain and she has never been the same since."

Just what I needed to cheer me up.

"You're very quiet, Philippa. Sorry, I shouldn't be going on like that."

"It's OK, Em. I'm feeling really sad. Not only did I love Flora, but she loved me. I'll miss that."

This was obviously too much for Emily. She changed the subject.

"I got your septic tank cleaned out. Condoms. Hundreds of them. The little gurrier who did it wanted to know how a woman on her own managed to get through them all."

"You should have told him I use them to protect my seedlings from frost."

Thank goodness Andy was taking precautions. Gloria was obviously a nymphomaniac. At least the rest of us feign the occasional headache just to pretend we're halfway normal.

"There's an archaeological trip to Clonmacnoise next week. Maybe it would help Letty to come and see all those grave slabs. Put things in perspective."

I didn't really understand the logic but nodded down the phone as I hung up.

Letty lit the fire while I made us a pot of tea. Just as we put our feet up, a voice called from the kitchen door. Andy. And Gloria.

"Just what we need! Under no circumstances offer them a caramel square or vanilla slice, Letty. I'll do some toast."

Gloria came into the room clutching a solanum in one hand and a bonsai in the other. She offered me the solanum.

"Thought you might need cheering up, Letty. This is a *Tree of Life* bonsai, to mark Flora's passing and returning."

I was impressed, in spite of myself. Dangerous to allow such feelings any houseroom.

"Have a seat," I suggested. "I'll make you some toast. The vanilla slices, etc. are off the menu."

Revenge is sweet.

I came back with a plateful of warm toast, dripping with raspberry jam. Letty was leaning on Gloria's shoulder, crying her heart out. Andy was on the other side, holding Letty's hand.

Life is full of surprises.

"It was meant to be, Letty," Gloria said in the tenderest of tones I'd heard outside a convent. "We can't do a blessed thing about it. The more you try to, the worse it gets. You just cry to your heart's content."

How come she had so little feeling for the cider

trees she'd lopped on her own farm? Perhaps Andy was having a civilising influence after all.

"*Those whom the Gods love die young,*" Andy declared as if for the first time. "Flora was much loved; she had a good life. And she's still around."

I slipped out and took Teddy from the travel bag and put him in Letty's arms.

"See what I mean," continued Andy. "Teddy even smells of Flora. Bet she'll come back as something even more beautiful."

Shortly, we were all in tears. I made a fresh pot of tea and handed round the caramel squares and vanilla slices. Who cares about revenge? Life is too short.

When they'd disappeared to whatever scratcher they'd found, I told Letty about the Clonmacnoise outing.

"Don't feel like doing anything," she said. "Even breathing is an effort. Wish I were dead."

"Well, you're not dead, Letty and that means you must stay alive. I insist you go. You might even enjoy yourself." Albeit unlikely. It wasn't really the weather for outings, but there was to be a celebration of the Epiphany in Ciaran's Chapel. Perhaps Letty would find some solace, some sort of release in religion. Stranger things have happened.

"Be the hard oul!" Seamus greeted me in his mock Dublin accent as we arrived at the Clonmacnoise carpark. I ignored his insult to my origins and merely replied.

"Seamus! Long time no see."

I'd forgotten how absence is such *sweet* sorrow. He was still clad in his grey suit with the shiny behind.

"Got over th'ole honeymoon in one piece?" His single entendre didn't raise a blush. Sex is more a hang-up for Seamus than it is for me. Noreen's ear was flapping. She came over to me.

"Don't mind him, Philippa. He doesn't mean any harm. Thinks it's all a great joke."

Sex is never a laughing matter. Fun but not funny. Unless you're arrested at the stage of development in which Seamus is imprisoned.

"Philippa!" Letty whispered. "I'll stay in the car. Can't face all these people."

Solitude. The slippery slope.

"Not on Letty. You must come. In this country it's illegal to sit in a locked car," I lied.

She got out heavily, clutching the oilskin bag with Teddy inside. God help Letty, not to mention the rest of us, if she ever lost that bag.

Emily arrived. She gave a nod in Letty's direction.

"She's so-so," I said. "You haven't enquired, but I'll tell you just the same – Emily, I've never felt more miserable in my life. It's as if I've lost my own child. I'm like a wounded animal flailing around for comfort."

"Sure you could have half a dozen before the eggs pack it in."

"Don't know, Emily. The humour seems to have gone off me."

We went ahead in crocodile after Seamus and Noreen, along the wood and wire fence. Seamus stopped at the wooden figure of the old famine woman, weeping.

"Sure, God help her. She could have been me own mother," he said.

Typical Irish sentimentality, wasting emotion on what's past, while hard hearts are brought to the present.

"That old wan! Hasn't she a good farm in the disadvantaged area with premium payments piling up in the bank," said Noreen, attempting to laugh but not quite succeeding. She got a dirty look from Seamus and folded her arms.

"No sign of the Greenes," Emily said, looking around. "Little Tommy had a bit of a cold at Christmas but they said they'd bring him. Believe Duncan sent the child a wonderful present. A toy helicopter that really works."

"Lucky child, surrounded by love."

"Not a bother on him. Beautiful. Very like Percy – but someone said if you live with horses, you take on their looks."

With any luck he'll forego the tassels on the shoes.

Just as we were about to enter the new coffee shop in the interpretative centre, a voice halloed. The Greenes, Gaye, Percy and offspring, in the latest McLaren buggy with fur-trimmed cover.

I felt Letty freeze at the sight of young Tommy. I wanted to tell her that the child was precious, conceived in desperation, every cell and pore cared for, loved. And not to be too angry. But she ran off, ahead of Seamus and Noreen.

"Pips! Great to see you." said Gaye, effervescent as usual. How I envy her energy. But then her heart is light with love.

"What a beautiful child, Gaye," I said with reverence before the most angelic, wise yet simple of faces. And he smiled, which is always endearing.

I made the usual, "polite" remarks. "What wonderful teeth! Very advanced for his age. What a big boy!" Though the child wouldn't thank me in another twenty years for that particular remark.

"Pippy," said Gaye, her face full of concern and sympathy. I almost crumpled then and there. "Really sorry to hear about Flora . . . Knowing you, you must have loved her – and she you."

I did crumple.

"Oh Gaye, that's maybe what killed her!" I let out a strangled cry that left my throat aching.

The rest of the Esker Archaeological Society had arrived and passed by into the Coffee Shop. The wind coming in off the Shannon was too bitter for the weak sun to make any impression. Cold seems to cloak sorrow better than a summer's day.

"Don't be daft, Philippa! Love never killed; it's the thing that keeps us all going. If we didn't love a plant in the house, giving it water and food, it would die. Just like the rest of us."

"But Flora died in spite of it all, all the tenderness on earth didn't keep her alive."

Gaye looked defeated for a second, recollected something and that bright sparkle returned.

"That's true, in a cruel twist of fate, but only because Flora used the independence love had given her and enabled her to explore. And that was her choice, as a free person. And the consequences were desperate."

Amen to that.

"I wrote a poem about it, Gaye." I fished in my bag for the lines I'd scribbled in the small hours of a sorrowful morning.

She'll feel no more the heat of the sun
Nor the wind on her face in the meadow
She'll see no more the colour of corn
Nor the swoop and dive of the swallow.
All the world is lost to her . . ."

"Oh, God, Pips, stop!"

We fell against each other, just as Percy and Dickie came round the corner arm in arm. They hesitated, and then hurriedly separated. Percy gave me the cheekiest wink I'd ever seen. Dickie blushed to the roots of his blond scalp.

"Gentlemen," I said, stiffly.

"There you are Percy-Plum," Gaye said. "Pippy's been telling me about Flora. Only three."

"Dreadful business," Percy said. "Just dreadful."

They both sailed past shaking their heads. We watched them walk towards the coffee shop.

"They've a really good relationship. Almost better than a man and woman would have."

Easily done when there's no rubbish to be put out or a bath to be cleaned.

The chill wind blew up from the lake again.

"I suppose we'd better enter the fray or be frozen to death," I said to Gaye.

I held the door of the coffee shop as she took off some of the paintwork with the wheels of the designer buggy. The rest of the gang were there: Seamus and Noreen ensconced before a plate of brown bread, mound of butter and several of those tasteless single servings of marmalade. Percy and Dickie were tucking into the same slice of cheesecake, a bored Emily looking on. She smiled when she saw me and came over to the counter with her tray.

"Nothing worth buying there, Philippa. You could pave a road with the Danish pastries and the boys said the cheesecake was out of a packet. Noreen and Seamus were sensible bringing their own bread."

I cast my eyes around the room in a panic. "Em, any sign of Letty?"

"There, behind the pillar. You never told me Andy was coming."

He didn't tell me either. Wanted to keep his acts of kindness to himself. Perhaps the good part of him was expanding. I wasn't going to hold my breath.

Emily put her tray on a table beside the window. "We're learning the oddest things on this women's course, Philippa. All about the myth of romantic love."

"Tell me more," I urged.

"Well, apparently there's a huge difference between 'falling in love' and 'being in love'."

Sounded somewhat familiar but I gave an encouraging grunt.

"The 'falling' bit is when we feel our knees turn to jelly, can't eat, or sleep, whereas 'being' means we really care about the other person, want what is best for them."

I racked my brain to work out which it was I felt for Gerald.

"What, Emily, if you happen to have a bit of both?"

She pulled at the combs keeping up her topknot.

"The books don't mention that!"

Emily handed me her Danish pastry and disappeared into a slough of despondency.

"Books don't have any answers, Em," I said gently. "We've to discover those for ourselves."

Much too difficult.

I looked towards Letty, her eyes red from recent crying. And at Andy whose face had a softness he rarely showed. There were no answers, only questions.

The announcement for the next audio-visual showing told us to take our seats. Emily and I swallowed our tea silently.

"About that love business," she said, pushing the crockery to one side, "I think the two kinds of love *are* connected but the second kind is more lasting. The first is only so we can experience the second. But some people never take the trouble."

I was sort of lost, but she seemed happy with that, so I left her to it. No sense in spoiling her neat rationale.

Andy looked at me as I passed.

"Hi, Sis. Glor was supposed to come but stayed in bed instead. Said she didn't like religious places."

"Thanks for looking after Letty so well. Drop in for a bite to eat on the way home."

"Happy to. Glor and I thought you needed a bit of a break. All been a bit of a strain for you. You look about ten years older."

Cheer me up some more.

In very poor drawings, the audio-visual show told of the building of Clonmacnoise, of raid upon raid on the rich monastery, of the violence done to its inhabitants. Nothing new on the face of the earth with invasions and killings everywhere. Tommy gurgled all through it and Letty sighed. When the lights went on again, Andy was busy easing a mound of soggy tissues under the seat in front.

We trooped down a corridor lined with scenes telling the same story, just in case we missed anything. The graveslabs had been moved here for safekeeping, a delightful collection of inscribed stones. After all of this, visiting the ruins seemed superfluous.

"You're very quiet," Emily crept up on me. "Noticed it since you've come back. The women's studies course says men take our voices from us, castrate our creativity."

"Really, Emily!" I laughed in spite of myself. "If there's any castrating to be done, I'll do it."

I debated whether to let Emily in on my thoughts or keep them safely hidden. A thought shared with one is a rumour in the neighbourhood.

"Well, Em, the truth is when I married Gerald I wanted a child very much. I assumed it went with the licence. But Gerald wasn't too keen. So, I throttled back somewhat. Then Flora fell into the void. I just couldn't leave her alone in the poverty Letty and she were in. No father, no money and no hope. And now she's gone . . . So, maybe your course is right. Maybe Gerald 'castrated' my wish to create a child."

"There's more than one way to skin a cat," Emily said enigmatically, as we put our feet over the portal into Teampall Ciaran.

The ceremony had just begun. The tiny choir of six children and one guitar were busy singing *Breathe on me breath of Christ*. I wished it were as simple as that, that "giving in", donating our lives to Christ solved everything. But, as Mohammed said: "Trust in God, but first tie your camel." Our mortal part in the proceedings is never clear.

With the ending of the hymn, the murmur of an old woman saying her rosary bounced off the stone walls. The priest, nonplussed, smiled a welcome.

"Dear Lord," he began, "we celebrate the coming of the Three Wise Men bringing the baby Jesus their gifts of gold, frankincense and myrrh, symbols of your kingship, divinity and death. And we celebrate Jesus showing himself to these three men as he showed himself to the world later."

The priest stopped to do something at the altar, and pat the great hank of hair to which the wind was showing huge disrespect. Clonmacnoise in the middle of winter is no place for the vain.

He turned to face us, his hair lifting like the roof of a shed in a storm. "And today we offer our thanks for the life of Ellen O'Reilly, the last parishioner to be buried in these sacred grounds."

"Just what we need," Emily nudged, her eyes towards Letty, standing blue and numb in the cold.

I wanted to tell Emily not to worry, that it didn't matter what occurred, Letty would find something in it to remind her of Flora. Beyond the far wall the chink of stone on spade could be heard as the diggers prepared the grave. The choir started up again. *Panis Angelicus* with a glorious soprano whose voice soared from the roofless church into the heavens above. Even the murmuring woman stopped and looked transfixed. Letty had something that looked not exactly like peace but certainly no pain on her face. Andy winked at me. Always irreverent. Gaye's little baby let out a primitive call of sorts, trying to join in the action. Percy and Dickie stood close together at the doorway, shadows carved in the weak sunlight. And I was alone, though not alone. Whatever the distance, I knew then that Gerald and I were twin souls; we had *plighted our troth* freely and truthfully. Nothing could alter that. Like Donne's compass points, we might be separated in time or place, but we were inextricably bound.

I left the ceremony just before it finished, as the choir sang *Christ be before me* and walked towards the harbour. A cruiser was mooring, casting ropes to the shore in the hope that one would cling and help them land. Seeing it was Christmas, I obligingly tied them to a bollard. A tiny, grey-haired woman with a sailor's hat smiled, "Jolly nice of you, bit of a swell just there." The "swell" was doing its best to climb the jetty and wet my shoes. A male of the species cut the engine and jumped ashore.

"Got her long?" He glanced at the sailor-hatted madame. "The boat," I emphasised.

"A year," he smiled as if congratulating himself. The cabin was freshly painted and the seating boasted new upholstery; a toytown sittingroom, complete with cat.

"Amazing how people crease themselves going for bigger and better houses, yet they'll happily spend weeks in cramped confinement on a boat," a voice from behind observed. Percy, looking almost handsome in the strong light from the lake, his eyes narrowed against the wind and spray. "Saw you sneak off from the incantations."

I bridled at "sneak". I had simply left.

"Quite right too," he said as if by way of apology. "Though Tommy enjoyed watching the old woman jangling her rosary. Might be worth getting him one." His feet shifted, tossing the tassels on his shoes. "Just like to say, you know, really tough about that little girl. The thought of losing Tommy would be . . ."

"I appreciate what you're saying, Percy," I said to put him out of his misery. Commiserating is one of the most difficult of arts.

"Do you? Do you really?" he asked more eagerly than I would have wished. I didn't want his happiness in the palm of my hand.

I nodded.

The two sailors were busy preparing what looked like either an omelette gone wrong or scrambled eggs. A tomato was being massacred to slivers. Teabags were tossed into a pot with gay abandon.

"Life goes on, Percy. No matter what happens. Just like the ants in a disturbed nest, we rush about mending here, re-building there, except it's mostly internal rents and cracks."

He looked at me with what I saw as real human feeling, almost love. He stretched out a hand.

"Must get back," he said, lightly pressing my arm. "There's some old dear they're planting. Better look willing."

The tassels on his shoes looked almost beautiful, tossing about in the wind.

A small group had gathered around the black hole in the earth. The last parishioner with permission to be buried in the hallowed grounds, along with saints and high kings. The priest had thrown his hair at it and let the weather do its worst with his mop. It had now fallen in hanks around his ears and onto his collar. He would have quite a job piecing it together again.

He blessed the grave and intoned the usual incantations to cast the evil spirits away. The coffin was lowered but no one came forward to toss in the first handful of clay and say goodbye. She had outlived her family and knew the fear of the old – "who will bury me?"

"This was a bad idea," Emily whispered, her eyes pinned on Letty sobbing for all she was worth, Teddy clutched tightly in her arms.

"It couldn't be better," Gaye said, "she has a ton of tears to shed."

"Death's a terrible thing." Emily took out an embroidered handkerchief and blew her nose.

I didn't like to tell her we'd all face it one day; sometimes it's more charitable to leave people with their illusions.

Andy led Letty away. The rest of us scattered to our various cars with promises of phone calls and visits.

"Sophia said to give you her best. She's a bad cold and had to forego the outing but she hopes to see you soon," Emily said climbing in beside Dickie.

I couldn't wait.

Unfortunately, Sophia didn't waste any time. On a particularly dismal evening she and Dahling, "just happened to be passing" and, in her usual poshspeak by Linguaphone, so becoming in one so beautiful, she wished me a happy New Year, "in spite of recent sadness." Dahling nodded, looking at the floor. They were dressed to kill with Sophia in a flowing midnight blue confection and Dahling in evening suit with a real bow tie.

"It's the Lysaght-Moore's usual New Year caper. Just a few friends," Sophia informed.

A mere fifty people. Nothing serious. However, I let her away with it, being too cold and tired to quibble.

"Such a *charming* Christmas we had. We went down to our old stomping ground at Ashford. The food is always reliable and the beds aired."

At £300 a night no more than you would expect. The tiny piece of membrane that usually kept the temper part of my hypothalamus in check decided to go thwang just at that instant.

"Heard it's gone off dreadfully. Everyone goes to *Mount Juliet* nowadays. Lots of exercise bicycles."

I could have sworn she sucked in her stomach a further notch. They left having barely touched their glasses of *Philippa's Phizz*, my decoction of elderflower and gin. The best cortex burner known. The evening was a glorious blur. Even Letty cheered up as I regaled her with my stories from the South of France.

I capitalised on Letty's turn for the better and hooked her onto the farm chores. Andy came to help.

"Really Pips, you can't expect Letty to go near those pigs!"

"Emily does. Of course, Emily has more guts than anyone knows about," I informed him. Who on earth would do a women's studies course unless they had the bravery of Jeanne d'Arc?

They looked at me, picked up the buckets of boiled vegetable waste and went quietly towards the pigs.

The three maiden gilts were now fully fledged mothers, well into their second pregnancy. Andy was busy experimenting as to the best way to preserve their offspring – wet versus dry curing. There were two sides languishing in an old bath in the barn and one half-way up the chimney being smoked to a cinder. I said nothing. Live and let live, I decided. Experience is the best teacher. Though it's a dreadful waste of a good piglet.

"Just saying to Letty how we should have some of the bacon that's nearly ready. And those cabbages you raised last summer are still holding up in the garden. How about that? Bacon and cabbage."

Can be greasy and tough but I kept my promise.

"Can't say I ever had it," Letty said. "Flora and me was so poor we lived on sausages. Never bought no big chunks of meat," Letty said, pulling out a well-used hanky.

I felt I was going to lose my rag, for once. Tell her enough was enough. But I knew for her it would never be. I left Andy to comfort her and took the pigs their dessert.

They smelt it miles away – three snouts were thrust through the electric wire at just the right angle to avoid a shock. Quivering and hoinking they stood up to their knees in mud, anticipation in every pore. I turfed the swill over into the trough and watched as they not so much ate it but sucked it to death. The noise of a pig at a trough has to be heard to be believed. What mothers say about people with bad table manners is true.

"Fair dinkum, eh?" Andy said, his colonial accent still showing. Letty had a slight trace of a smile as she stared enraptured at the wrecking crew.

"They certainly look in the pink, which is more than can be said for their paddock," I said.

Hardly a square inch of ground was left undisturbed. Nothing green or brown remained. Even the brambles had been massacred to within an inch of their life. The wallow was like a small pond.

"We'll have to move them, Andy," I decided. He rubbed his head.

"Where to?" he asked, his arms outstretched.

"We'll rent some woodland from PJ," my neighbour and critic. Andy shrugged his shoulders.

PJ was agreeable, especially when I paid him in advance. In the morning we bucket led them towards their new hunting ground and pulled their arks with the tractor and rope. They squealed with pleasure at the sight of the scratching posts and within minutes had the wood creaking. PJ looked me straight in the eye, opened his mouth to say something and wisely kept quiet. I have him trained at last.

We had a slight celebration that night. Glorry had decided to return to the Mendips to "tidy up a few loose ends." Letty and I gathered that money featured somewhere.

"Maybe she and Andy are thinking of buying a farm," Letty let slip and then denied all knowledge of it when I asked for more information.

"Well, Letty let's hope it's as far from here as it is possible to get, somewhere you need a canoe to get to the mainland and even then you've to wait a month for a mail ship – what with a dead cow, piglet and goodness knows how many empty bottles of elderberry wine, I think I've borne more than humanly possible!"

"Of course," was all she said. Letty can be cheeky at times.

However, they didn't come empty handed. Andy planted a bottle of whisky on the table and Gloria opened a gigantic bag of pistachio nuts. An abomination. You deserve a medal or at least more than a miserable nut when you've managed to extricate them from their shell.

We started with bite sized portions of vol-au-vents, filled with minced lamb, onion and carrot in a rich, creamy sauce. It was when we moved onto the beef olives that I took a *crise* and thought of and missed Gerald with such an ache it was like being severed with a machete. Beef olives are Gerald's absolute favourite. They had a hollow ring without his appreciation, without his presence, without his love.

"No thanks, Andy. You help yourselves. I've got a bit of a sore head," I lied, up to a point. I left them to it and went to bed. I had the phone in my hand before I had time to think. I could almost taste its hollow ring in the corridors of Woodleigh.

"Woodleigh. Good evening," a voice like Pimmsy answered.

I returned the greeting.

"Why, Philippa! Where on earth did you go to? Haven't had a decent bite to eat since you left. Hang on till I get that young whipper-snapper."

Praise indeed. And he sounded sober. Something was wrong.

"Pips! Nothing wrong? No, of course there doesn't have to be anything wrong for you to ring – though it *is* your first time since you left."

"If it weren't for the beef olives I'd have been fine – after all, it's only been a fortnight. It's just . . ."

"So, I've an old beef olive to thank for this attack of . . . whatever it is."

We were silent for a moment after that and then I remembered how much a phone call to England cost.

"When are you coming over? And how come Pimmsy isn't his usual form?"

"Well, quite a lot has happened in that quarter. There was a slight altercation in the camp. Pim – I mean Pop was on his usual evening meander down the driveway when Mortimer came from across the park on his horse. Winged him. Arm broken in three places. Pop hasn't touched a drop since and Mortimer has been banned for life from the estate. Amazing the change in atmosphere. It's like spring has arrived early."

"Pity it hadn't happened sooner."

"Is it really too late for you, Philippa? You couldn't see yourself installed in full control?"

"No. It wouldn't be me. It's part of other people's past. I'm happier here."

"So, that's it?"

I let him draw his own conclusions.

"Pity you hadn't all this worked out *before* we married. It would have made life easier."

"Pity you didn't let me know what the Ransomes *chez eux* were like. I'd no idea life could be so miserable. And you were so busy with your writing. There was nowhere to turn for comfort."

"Pips, you make that sound really awful."

Oh, but it was. However, I'd no intention of appearing pathetic and weak, admitting to my flabby upper lip.

"You still there?"

"Of course. What's the weather like?"

He cradled the phone gently. How dare he! It was my call.

Monday was a day I usually looked forward to after the indulgences of the weekend – the extra glass of wine when one shouldn't really and the half pound or so of cheese on oat biscuits when one's embroidery wouldn't behave itself. However, *that* Monday, I hated it. Being alive was torment, a blank wall of pointless chores like washing clothes and scrubbing the floor. Perhaps a child to look after, to coo at, dress up and bring out to see the bare trees and feel the air on its face . . .

Letty was like Banquo's ghost, all white and lifeless. I could see she wanted to die, merely waking up was a heartbreak because reality would always be the same – no Flora.

In desperation I phoned Emily. Always sobering to hear other people's problems; our own never seem quite so desperate.

"Just on my way out – to my women's studies class," she gasped for air. I envied her busyness. "Funnily enough, I was going to drop in to see you on my way, that's why I'm a bit early, so put the kettle on – water, not brandy this time."

Em had obviously lost her sense of fun.

She was tootling up the driveway in minutes. A new Emily emerged from her little toy car.

"Emily, you've had your hair done! And new earrings!"

A bunch of golden coils hung from her earlobes almost to her collar bone, glinting in the morning light like a saint's halo. They cheered me up at once. I wanted to hug her but restrained myself. Emily is *la femme conventionelle*.

"'Be yourself, indulge those feelings, pay attention to your own wants', all these feminist books say. We should no longer be defined by our role but by our personality," she almost shouted with an energy I'd never seen in her before. "None of which is new to you, Philippa, but what a revelation to the rest of us! Maisie McDonald, who's sixty if she's a day, burst into tears when she realised she'd done nothing for herself and her life was nearly over. I told Dickie it was either me or the onions – nothing new, except this time I meant it and," she leaned towards me, "for the first time, I didn't care about the consequences. I couldn't bear it the way it was. It's really better to know where you stand."

Brave, brave Emily. Reality is what sends most of us reaching for the gin or the biscuit tin.

"And what was his reply, Emily?"

"Just looked at me as if I were mad. Asked me when the course was finished. I told him it never finished, after this one there would be another and another. I knew what he was getting at, blaming something else."

"And?"

"Well, so far, he's been keeping a low profile and I haven't seen an onion for at least 48 hours," she waggled her earrings. "Speaking of seeing things, Philippa, what about you and Gerald? Noreen has some garbled story, I needn't tell you and Sophia keeps talking about a 'tragedy'."

"At least I'm still keeping the tongues wagging. Thought I'd lost my touch. Fact is, Em, I just can't live in Woodleigh. I had to preserve my sanity, though it's not easy. Once you've known intimacy," Emily started at the mention of the word, "I don't necessarily mean anything, you know, to do with the flesh – though that too – more the 'communion' of like minds, life is a lot duller."

Emily leaned back in her chair and sighed.

"I know exactly what you mean, though I don't know if I've ever felt it. Perhaps I *will* have that brandy after all."

"No, Em. With all due respect, that's the slippery slope you must avoid. Go on to your class, be you, examine your life. A brandy will merely take the edge off the pain for an hour or two."

"You're so . . . strong, Philippa."

I followed her to the door and before she stepped into her car I gave her that hug. I hoped she knew the road well enough not to be blinded by her tears.

Typical. Help the whole world, Philippa, but who helps you?

"Is she gone?" Letty put her head round the door. "Just couldn't face anything human."

So much for me.

"Oh, I don't mean you, Philippa. You've been so . . . well, you've been the best friend I ever had, apart from Flora. But then Flora was like another skin, part of me. Sorry. I'm just not great today."

"I really understand, Letty. I know it must be really hard for you. It's hard for me too." No harm in letting her know the truth. "In fact, though it's the one thing I've wanted ever since I got married, I've decided to put off having children – just yet. It all sounds like dreadful suffering."

Letty sat down, really looking at me for the first time in weeks.

"Pity you feel like that Philippa. Flora was best thing ever 'appened to me. Wouldn't swap having her for anything – she was an angel. But I do wish she weren't . . . gone. Keep wanting to dig her up, just to make sure. But Andy says her spirit's alive. So that keeps me going."

"Well, I've made up my mind about children, Letty. I'm just not ready for any disaster that may befall. And with Gerald not around, it's all so unsettled."

In fact, I'd decided to definitely eliminate any possibility of children for the moment.

"You two not speaking?"

"On the surface, we're at sixes and sevens but underneath, we'll always feel the same way. Nothing will change that. In the heel of the hunt, Letty, love is an act of will."

She looked puzzled but then Letty thinks that love is something that happens to you, like a dose of measles. For some, it vanishes as quickly.

"Wonder if Gloria's coming back?"

"What on earth makes you doubt it?" And just when I was beginning to feel something akin to humane towards her. Never considerate was our Gloria.

"Well, she hasn't phoned once."

"Don't worry Letty, Gloria knows when she's well off. Besides, would you forgive her for lopping your cider orchard if you were Hank?"

She stared into the fire, hugging Teddy. Whoever invented Teddy should receive a medal – saviour of the human race, balm of hurt minds.

Phone.

"Thought I'd ring to apologise for my precipitate departure the other evening. I suppose I've a lot on my plate and without you, Philippa, life seems so much more bleak." Gerald's voice caressed me down the wires. I succumbed abysmally.

"Don't worry your head. I understand," I lied. He was silent for a telling moment or two. To Gerald I am like a fish in a goldfish bowl – visible from all sides.

"I'd just like to say 'I'm sorry' for the Ransomes, for Woodleigh, for all the petty meanness you had to put up with."

"That's a help," I admitted.

"So, I've had a good long think and chat with Father. I've decided to take a short holiday and come to see you."

Taken aback, I didn't know whether to be pleased or sorry. There was the tug of love, of nights of rupture but there was the untidiness of it all. Alone, life is simple; with another it's one hundred percent more complicated.

"Well, for goodness sake, Philippa, don't set the phone lines on fire with enthusiasm."

"I was just thinking what bedroom I'd put you in – Letty's in the pink one. But of course, it will be mine – seeing we're married."

"Sometimes, Philippa . . . So, I should be over by the weekend."

I hadn't a moment to lose.

The following morning I took myself off to Dublin for a non-intrusive, ecologically sound but reliable device to ensure that Gerald's sperm and my little egg didn't shake hands.

Women searching for such devices do so in some slight luxury nowadays. Grimy hallways, full of screaming children and queues out the door are a thing of the past. Competition has brought plush carpets and pleasant receptionists.

"May I help you?" she asked with mock sincerity. I can see through anything.

"Could I have a chat with one of your contraceptive experts?"

"There's a five minute delay this morning, if you don't mind waiting. I'll bring you coffee/tea?"

Anything to keep you here. It was a nice thought, but Bewley's was already a treat on my agenda.

"I'll just have a gander at a magazine."

I sat beside a dark-haired woman with a crew cut hairdo. She glowered at me.

Perhaps I should have had accepted that cup of tea.

I protected myself with a glossy magazine, opening it on a intriguing article entitled "Hormones for Free," about women's experiences of eating their placenta after childbirth: one woman chilled hers and ate it with some slices of beetroot on a bed of iceberg lettuce; another fried it with onions. Put you off children, food and liver for life, not necessarily in that order.

"You *did* want to see the doctor?" the anxious, sincerely insincere receptionist enquired.

I was certainly torn between knowing whether these women survived this *entrée de placenta* and wondering whether to get the whole kit and kaboddle sewn up, once and for all. Life would be so much simpler, though I expect one would have to cauterise the hypothalamus too.

I followed her down the carpeted corridor, past white rooms that smelled of lavender. Not a picture of a baby in sight. Ovaries are superfluous, one of nature's inconveniences like breast milk and eggs and sperm. What would Simey say about it all? Is this his spirituality – sex without the responsibility?

"The doctor will be with you shortly, if you would like to take a seat."

No sooner had one door closed than another opened. A black woman in a white coat greeted me.

"What can I do for you, sister?"

I laughed.

"Under the skin, of course," she added. A doctor with a sense of humour! A rare specimen.

She looked enquiringly. "I'm sure you're not just here to shoot the breeze," she smiled. "What had you in mind?"

I explained in detail.

"Something that will do the trick – preferably, though without hormones or chemicals."

She listened impassively.

"The coil would not be suitable for you if you haven't had any children – just in case there was any damage done to the fallopian tubes."

Delightful.

"Sounds like either a diaphragm or a cap – the difference being one is less reliable but the other is more difficult to insert."

The oldest device invented, one step up from the half lemon of the Romans – squeezed, of course, the acid acting as a sperm killer for the acrobatic ones that managed to claw their way over the side of the lemon. However, if they managed that, they deserved to win.

She reached into a deep drawer and drew out a card with a selection of rubber domes tied on with pieces of elastic. She extracted one.

"The idea is this little thing stays glued to the cervix so the little swimmers can't climb up into the fallops and join up with an egg. However, getting it up there can take a little practice. While you're doing that, I'll do some tests if you would oblige me with . . ." She handed me a kidney dish.

Clutching charts and samples, she left me to it . . .

"See you shortly – and the best of luck."

I needed every ounce of it. Along the straight and narrow passage the piece of rubber slid beautifully, but as soon as it hit the space above, it sensed freedom, did a somersault and wanted to come back down. For the first time in my life I discovered my fingers weren't long enough to reach anywhere meaningful. Only by doing a foetal curl and shoving my hand half way up my innermost parts could I manage. It was definitely easier getting pregnant.

"Good, good," the rubber merchant said on her return. "We've got suction there. Nothing will get past that, though it's a bit like bolting the stable door," she said as she examined my chart.

"I wasn't aware we were discussing horses," I smiled my most polite smile.

"In a manner of speaking," she said, grasping her speculum with energy. "Haven't been a bit peaky of late? Slightly dizzy? Nauseous?"

"No more than usual."

✇ *Chapter Eleven* ✇

As soon as I reached home I asked Letty to put the kettle on.

"Fancy a little tipple with it after your trying day in the city?"

"Certainly not, Letty!"

She looked at me as if I had forty heads.

"That bad, was it?"

"I'd a perfectly nice day, thank you. Just slightly tired and . . . dazed."

I pulled out the tapestry footstool that cost an absolute mint and laid my feet on it. I could have sworn they were swollen.

"Kettle's boiled," Letty shouted from the kitchen. "Tea, coffee?"

"Herbal tea, please, Letty. Raspberry leaf." I shouted back.

She came running into the room. Letty can be tiresome.

"Gall bladder playing you up?" she asked.

"No, Letitia. I'm perfectly all right. Just needing a refreshing drink."

A large gin wouldn't go amiss, but I restrained myself.

"So, what's new in the big smoke?" Letty handed me the steaming mug of raspberry tea.

"Can't say I noticed anything," I said. Shock I suppose. I sipped the tea slowly and eased off my shoes. "Though a lot of people seem to be cannibalising their placenta."

"Their what?"

The kitchen door slammed. Letty looked up.

"It's Andy."

"Hi do, Sis. Bit peaky are we?"

I held back a scream. Perhaps Woodleigh wasn't the worst place on earth after all.

"Speaking of peaky, haven't seen Gloria lately."

"Neither have I, Sis. Haven't seen hide nor hair of her since she went back to scrounge some money from Hank."

"You're not worried he hasn't taken a hatchet to her in revenge."

"Didn't know you cared, Pips," he gave a sly grin at Letty.

"I saw that, Andrew. I'm mildly concerned, that's all."

Letty brought him a steaming mug of coffee. He took a large brown envelope from inside his sheepskin jacket.

"Got that photo done, Let." He handed her a large photograph framed in limed ash.

Letty collapsed onto the couch.

"You'll ruin it with those tears, Letty," I sighed.

Andy looked at me sharply. "Sometimes, Sis, you can be just a bit too . . . much." He ran to Letty's side.

Didn't anyone realise how wretched *I* felt. How lonely and bereft?

"It's Flora," Letty held out the photograph.

Flora lay on her deathbed, a crown of white flowers on her head, her tiny hands folded across her chest. Eyes firmly closed. Like Rosetti's Ophelia, in another realm.

"My God, Andy, why on earth did you get that done?"

"Letty wanted it."

"But it's a travesty of Flora's life! She should be remembered for herself, her joy, her very self. Not this body lying dead."

I was so cross I didn't trust myself to stay any longer. I left them to it and went to bed.

Gerald, Gerald where are you?

Dawn was no improvement. Though six o'clock in the morning, Letty still had her light on to keep the ghosts at bay; at least sleep was knitting up her ravelled sleeve of care, judging by her snores. Why does death have to spoil everything? The ultimate cul-de-sac. I envied animals' acceptance of it. Their fight for life is more important than the dwelling on death, as the tougher bonhams push the weaker from the teat, or sheep climb over their dead companion to reach the juicy turnip.

The phone was ringing in Woodleigh before I realised what I was doing. The answering machine. I left a rude message, made myself some hot chocolate instead of the steaming whiskey I'd have preferred and went back to bed.

Seconds later Letty woke me.

"What is it?"

"No need to bite my head off. It's ten o'clock after all! A phone call. Your husband."

She slammed the door.

I lifted the extension.

"Pips! Anything wrong?"

"Of course not! What on earth makes you think that?"

"Your call at the crack of dawn and the tone of your voice on the answering machine."

The phone was not the place for revelations.

"Hello, anybody there?"

"Yes. I heard you. My apologies for disturbing you."

"For goodness sake, Pippy, we're married, we've a right to disturb each other. We're bound together for better or worse. No one put a gun to our head."

I made an effort to pull myself together, to gather the shreds of my insides into some shape.

"I suppose I felt a bit lonely. Wanted to talk to someone vaguely human."

"That little sting tells me a huge amount. Oh, Pips! You're in a bad way. Wish I was there to help you, to squeeze you against my manly chest and say 'there, there'."

I fought against telling him where such demonstrations can lead.

"Don't worry, Gerald. I'm fine, really. I just had a bad night."

"Letty getting you down? Can be very trying being with someone who's grieving, without realising it."

"Andy's being very good, for once. He doesn't seem to mind her talking about it endlessly. Says he came to terms with death living with the aborigines. He believes in reincarnation. Says Flora is either a bird or a fish. Letty's joined the anti-hunting, shooting and fishing brigade. Spends hours on the phone and has offered to write letters to ministers and take part in protest marches."

"And what about you, Pips? How are you and Flora getting along?"

"I'm still very sad about losing her, as she was. I'm trying to think of her as changed into some other form. I want to believe it, so perhaps I will, though she'll always be part of me."

It was Gerald's turn to be silent.

"But here I am going on about myself – how about you and the folks around Woodleigh?"

"They're much the same. About to kick Mr Hazlett out and put Gladys in charge of everything. That woman has really come into her own. It's as if a key has been turned and the mechanism has become animated."

Wonderful what a good sexual life can do for a person.

"Apart from that, nothing strange. We're looking around for someone to run the farm. We need someone young and energetic, someone we can trust not to dip into the coffers, who's prepared to take a few risks.

By the way, that brother of yours, did he ever find a suitable outlet for his talents?"

"That's the best news I've heard all day. It never occurred to me; I must be slipping."

"I'll leave it to you to arrange."

Nothing to it.

"Gee whiz, Sis! The size don't matter a tinkers. Look at the size of the outback, for Crissake. The possibilities are endless."

"The bottom line is that the estate must survive, Andrew," I warned, in case he got carried away. "People depend on it for their livelihood."

"You trying to teach your brother how to suck an egg?"

"We won't mention ostrich ventures, shall we! And for goodness sake, tell no one over there about it. Free range chickens, if you're keen on feathered things, just might turn a penny or two."

He gave me another of his egg sucking looks.

"Letty'll come too. She'll be nearer Flora and she knows the place."

"Really, Andy. Every female I've brought into this house you've managed to inveigle yourself into their graces. What about dearest Glorry? Remember? The one who was such a 'sweet, nature-loving person' among other things?"

"Well, she's gone, ain't she?"

"No good reason to hitch onto the next thing in or out of tights!"

"Don't see why not, if one person needs the other and no one's complaining."

Who could argue with that?

Gerald arrived with the first spring sunshine and shoots of lords and ladies.

We hugged for an age and unglued ourselves only to climb into the car. I left the wheel to him. Just so he could get used to being in charge. I planned to retire from life, from the struggle, allow myself be tossed about like flotsam and jetsam – for a month or two anyway.

"You had me worried," he said, appraising me with that shining smile that would melt snow off a ditch. "But you look . . . wonderful."

What an amazing thing love is! We can feel

unlovable ourselves but it doesn't seem to stop anyone from feeling the opposite.

"You won't miss Woodleigh too much?"

"I'd be a liar if I said I wouldn't at all. But if you're not there, it's not the same. Pity."

"What is it about the place you like?" I asked the question that had intrigued me for months. He stared thoughtfully into the middle distance.

"I don't really know. Maybe the sweep of the gardens and trees towards the lake in the early morning with the merest hint of mist, the smell of earth and ripe fruit in the walled garden, or perhaps the sight of flames licking up the sittingroom chimney from the driveway. Who knows? Maybe all of these things, maybe something else: just the fact of being there."

"Well, this will be our humble abode for the nonce. A bit more cramped than Woodleigh but . . ."

"You're here, that's what's important."

I melted, as usual.

A hungry Poppy bellowed at our arrival.

"I'd better hurry and feed everyone before it's dark. Andy and Letty left for Aggie and Eddie in Limerick last night, to say their goodbyes."

"Here. Let me help. You're not alone any more."

"Not *entirely* alone."

"Thought you said Letty and Andy had gone?"

I took a deep breath.

"There's still someone else."

"For goodness sake, Philippa, what other skeletons are about to creep from your cupboard!"

I said nothing.

"Oh, the silent treatment now. Come over here Philippa! At once!"

Whatever power the male voice had on my central nervous system, I meekly submitted.

"Come on, you can tell me. I'll still love you – albeit with some slight difficulty. But don't let that worry you."

Oh, but it does, it does.

"Gerald, while I finish outside, if you wouldn't mind going in and putting the kettle on, lighting the range and sticking the casserole that's on the table . . ."

"Yes, dear. Right away, if not sooner."

The honeymoon was definitely over.

I tossed an armful of hay to Poppy and breathed in her warm, milky breath, superior to any perfume. Her calf gave me a desultory glance. But somehow, the pleasure had gone out of it all, the intense feeling of pleasure.

"Back so soon?" Gerald asked, up to his arm pits in ash, kindling and turf. "Afraid I haven't nearly finished *my* chores."

"I forgive you."

"Everyone out there all right?"

"Yes. Right as rain."

He was beside me in seconds. No point in beating around the bush.

"Gerald, remember you mentioned something about skeletons in the cupboard?"

"Yes."

"Well, there is something, someone, I mean who's coming to stay with us."

Why do we have to tell each other things, why can't people just guess!

"They're a bit small, at the moment, but in a few months' time, they'll be able for the rigours of life *chez nous*, all going well."

Still not a flicker.

"Gerald! I'm expecting a baby!"

"I could have told you that! I can give you the precise time of conception and the date of birth."

"How on earth did you know?"

"I was there when it happened!"

"How could I ever forget . . ."